CLUTCHED IN A VELVET TALON

A healthy morning and strong day to you, my lord and liege! I, Sir Juan Elabaro Hustin de Jericho, shall endeavor to clarify the many mysteries and enigmas surrounding the lands of the Hazat, my house and family. I do this with a heart made gladder by the knowledge that what I do benefits all humanity. While I have made my pledge to you, lord of all peoples, I still feel a debt to my own Royal House, that which bore me and gave me the strength necessary to serve your monumental goals. I would not reveal what I do here if I did not think it would benefit the Hazat as well as you. An understanding of our ways can dispel much of the ignorance that poisons relationships. While I cannot reveal all without betraying certain trusts, not everything should stay hidden, either. With these truths always at the fore of my thoughts, I look forward to answering some of the many questions the curious have about my house and its lands.

My fellow Hazat have long sought the best for all humanity. While we opposed you to the last, we did so out of a belief in our own ability to guide humanity into the 51st century. Your success in glorious battle, as well as your honor in victory, has lead more and more Hazat to respond to your majestic reign. Some of those who criticized me when I first entered your service now praise you, and their scions seek entry into the ranks of the Questing Knights. I like to think that my own service as one of the Emperor's first knights, especially my helping destroy the vile Fatar of Malignatius, helped change noble minds about your worthy endeavors.

I have always cherished the opportunity you gave me, a landless knight from a slandered family. Despite rumors of my parents' cowardice before the Battle of Fort Omala, you knighted me yourself shortly after your coronation, and ever since I have endeavored to serve you with all my heart and soul. Thus, when you gave me leave to seek out the truth of my parents' history, I readily accepted your request to also document my travels among the beautiful worlds of my youth. As you noted, these would not be secret plans for invading my family's worlds, but rather a vehicle to encourage appreciation of Hazat culture and ways among all people.

Other knights who conducted similar surveys, especially Baron Geoffrey Hawkwood, proved especially helpful when I began my preparations. As he had just returned from a similar tour of Hawkwood worlds, he overflowed with helpful comments and tips. Among his most valuable suggestions was to travel only with those companions most indispensable, to travel light and to dedicate my trip to both the Emperor and the Pancreator. Perhaps Baron Geoffrey's most helpful recommendation, however, was to forget that which I already thought I knew about the lands of my childhood. He believes that those who see fresh see best, and I quickly learned the truth of his conviction. I have tried to describe what I have seen without bias, though events of the past I can only repeat as I learned them. I did get a Hazat scholar to help me with the various histories, however.

My journey took me to the three jewels of the Hazat: Sutek, Aragon and Vera Cruz, as well as strife-torn Hira, site of my family's alleged ignominy. Along the way, I saw the splendor of these worlds anew, for their beauty shines like the multihued light of Hiran inferno coral. I also saw gloom and suffering I never before noticed, for many of our people live in squalor. I saw the crumbling slums of Sutek, the violent barrios of Aragon, and refugee camps on Hira. Even lovely Vera Cruz, untouched by war for centuries, has its pockets of poverty, and the troops in transit to and from Hira have become magnets for the worst human parasites.

I shall endeavor, my lord, to present all these features as they appeared to me, from the resplendent beauty of Castle Furias to the devastation of an artillery attack on a Hiran village, with all the honesty and objectivity my pen can yield. In the end, I hope all readers of this manuscript learn what it means to be Hazat.

Your humble servant,
Sir Juan Elabaro Hustin de Jericho

Sutek

Only Holy Terra itself has a longer history for the human race, and I can picture the excitement ancient explorers must have felt setting foot on a planet in a new solar system. We can only imagine the dreams it fulfilled and the opportunities it presented. Only imagination can serve us here, since Sutek's glory has faded much like the suns themselves.

History

My father once told me that you can see all of humanity's mistakes in Sutek's ruins, for they date back to our species' first hesitant steps beyond our birth system. Colonization of Sutek (then known as Sathra's Boon) began with high hopes, but these faded faster than a Scraver in daylight. The earliest domed communities (covered to protect against diseases in the air they had not yet cured) sprang up almost overnight, and collapsed just as quickly during the Sathra Rebellion. First zaibatsu guns and then desperate survivors tore apart the gleaming domes, and huge armies of Terran troops flooded over the planet. General (later Governor) Abdel Naguib led the occupation and reconstruction of the planet, and my nana told me he renamed the world Sutek after an ancient Terran myth.

Hastily constructed pioneer dwellings took the place of the old domes, and these grew quickly in the years after the rebellion. The First Republic used Sutek as the testing ground for a huge variety of experiments, including construction materials. Anything that they might get in trouble for using on Terra first saw testing on Sutek. Unstable bricks, cyberconcrete, genetically altered wood, self-heating plastics and more were put to use here, and all caused problems. The bricks broke down, cyberconcrete attacked its owners, genetically altered wood spawned new diseases, and self-heating plastic went haywire, melting both itself and its owners during the winter.

Most of these have disappeared under the dust of ages, though remnants are still visible. Modern buildings sometimes incorporate old materials. Palamedes himself dedicated St. Esmerelda's Cathedral on top of a Sathraist stronghold — Hoffman's Bluff on Pleroma — and consecrated the pre-existing parts to the Pancreator. The cathedral has always served as a center for theurgical studies. While not as notable as the schools on Holy Terra or Pentateuch, it has its share of famous (and infamous) alumni.

Even after the rebellion, the remaining buildings housed a growing discontent, and as the First Republic crumbled, more and more people left the zaibatsu-constructed cities for native dwellings. In the process, they uncovered more and more signs of Anunnaki occupancy, as well as indications that the zaibatsu had tried to exploit these ruins as secretly as possible. Sutek's most common conflicts during the Diaspora revolved around these sites, with different groups laying claim to whichever ones seemed most important. Some of these wars caused extreme devastation, especially those between the various Anunnaki worship cults that sprang up while House Chauki ruled the world. Thankfully, the Church stamped these out during its earliest days, but farmers still occasionally find demonic relics when plowing their fields.

House Chauki laid claim to the planet during the later years of the Diaspora. Its weak reign did little to prevent an overwhelming migration to the planet, with masses of humanity stopping at Sutek after fleeing Holy Terra. Conditions on Sutek, while never as bad as those on Terra, degenerated with the flood of refugees. Hunger and plague relentlessly stalked the planet.

Many of the sites also suffered severe damage during the wars, and most of the Anunnaki traces that once graced Sutek have been stolen, broken or destroyed. The Second Republic made some efforts to preserve what was left, but by the time of its well-deserved fall, soulless corporations had seized even these. Now my relatives do their best to maintain what is left for study by Church scholars, and prevent their misuse by forces of darkness.

Sutek grew substantially during the Second Republic, but its pride grew even more quickly than its population. Its proximity to Byzantium Secundus made it prone to democratic influences, and many corporations made their homes here. My ancestors either stepped aside to avoid this new force or else became sucked into it, committing the same sins as the corporate overlords. While rarely known for technological innovation, Sutek became a key world for the deal making that became so prevalent near the end of the Second Republic. As corporation gobbled up corporation, lawyers and financiers flocked to the planet. The planet's elite lived lives of unparalleled wealth and pleasure, but the average citizen found it difficult to hold the most basic of jobs before their employer disappeared into a new merger. They turned to any solace they could, including a variety of heretical cults. Padre Javier Eusebio, a prominent missionary of the time, once said, "To be from Sutek means to be an agent of evil – either a cultist, a banker or a lawyer."

As if in holy retribution for their crimes, the forces of the Second Republic suffered heavily on Sutek. Much of the planet depended on the dole for survival. The destruction of the welfare system left the planet in utter turmoil. Millions

of people had no idea where their next meal would come from. While the planet had a thriving food industry, including ranching, farming and the great yeast vats of Scarabi, most people lived in massive industrial centers like Djehut, Ashmunen and others. Before the Republican government moved to replace the welfare system, rumors of famine traveled from city to city. Looting broke out in Djehut and spread quickly across the planet. While rioters targeted the food markets first, their attentions soon grew to encompass whole cities.

Ironically, the richest farms remained untouched. My own ancestors and some other nobles owned these, and they theorized that the urban anarchists never knew of the riches in the wilds. The upheaval took months to die down, during which time my family began its righteous crusade against House Chauki. By the time the riots ended, much of what the looters sought lay broken around them, but my family could now help them.

During this time of troubles, the Hazat had sought out those Chauki who held positions of power on the planet. House Chauki did little to end the suffering of Sutek's people, preferring to use its might to prop up the heretical Second Republic. While they squandered Sutek's wealth, sending aid to Byzantium Secundus, the Hazat did what we could for our own people, helping them survive as best we could. When the rioting died down, famine and disease followed. These provided the final blows against Second Republic rule on the planet — as well as House Chauki.

The Rogue Worlders' attack on Byzantium Secundus ensured that no aid could come from the Second Republic. The Hazat moved in its stead, determined to save Sutek from both the plagues and rebels. The Church also did its best for our citizens, but providing for Holy Terra alone overtaxed its resources. Archbishop Desidere Muhan objected when my house declared Sutek a Hazat protectorate, but the people rejoiced.

At the same time, the Hazat and other noble houses moved against the raiders holding Byzantium Secundus. While Aragon was our main staging area, Sutek also played a part, though its role grew right after the battle. Many of the Rogue Worlders and their alien accomplices sought to flee past Sutek, aiming for our world and beyond. Sutek was sorely pressed to battle them, but battle them my ancestors did. They forced the attackers back through the jumpgate and into the dustbin of history.

Their next great task involved bringing the entire planet under one banner. House Chauki, while one of the planet's leading powers, never ruled the entire world. Merchant interests still maintained a great deal of power here. Nils De Vatha and the nascent Charioteers Guild took over Apollo Industries' jumpgate monopoly right under the Chaukis' noses. Embarrassed and desperate for some way to battle

Sutek Traits

Cathedral: Eskatonic (St. Esmerelda's in Djehut)
Agora: Scraver (in Djehut)
Garrison: 6
Capital: Djehut
Jumps: 1
Adjacent Systems: Byzantium Secundus, Vera Cruz (nightside), Holy Terra (nightside)
Solar System: Mercury II (.497 AU), Dominey (.773 AU, 2 moons), Cregstar (.886 AU), Sutek (1.13 AU, 2 moons), Yharit (5.071 AU), Kastaga (11.591 AU), Twenty-Something (34.303 AU, 23 moons), Exelon (74 AU), Jumpgate (74.123 AU)
Tech: 5
Human Population: 1.27 billion
Alien Population: 2 million Ur Obun, 1 million Ur Ukar, 500,000 others
Resources: Grapes, ruins, ancient materials
Exports: Processed foods, wines, industrial goods, laborers
Landscape: Pleroma, Sutek's dominant land mass, ranges from heavy tundra in the north to jungle in the south. Several large deserts also cut through it, but most of the continent is arable land. However, much of this land is at risk of becoming desolate as overfarming threatens to turn it into a giant dust mound. Additionally, the planet has been cooling since its sun began fading.

my ancestors, the Chaukis tried to seize the Charioteer's assets on Sutek and Byzantium Secundus.

The Charioteers responded at once with a blockade of Sutek, raids against Chauki shipping and appeals to potential allies. After several skirmishes, House Chauki found itself unable to ferry troops on or off the planet, and its allies on other worlds began suffering. By the time Princess Anyanwu Chauki backed down, her house was in disarray across the Known Worlds.

The Scravers also held a great deal of power on Sutek. The groups that would form this guild had a deep-seated interest in the world, with its Anunnaki ruins and the hoards of people crowded in its urban metropolises. While neither they nor the Charioteers ever made a bid for planetary control, their support proved crucial in our liberating the world from the Chaukis. The Charioteers had severely weakened House Chauki's interstellar network, and the Scravers proceeded to weaken their on-planet forces with sneak attacks, bribes and blackmail. When the time came, our forces had little trouble taking the planet and then hunting down the cowardly Chauki who tried to flee our noble wrath.

3

Then came the long process of rebuilding Sutek. My cousins in the Castenda branch of the family took the lead here. Their connections with the Scravers had proven invaluable in freeing the planet, and they also helped in repairing the damage of the upheaval. With Scraver assistance, the Castendas took control of the remaining Anunnaki sites in order to safeguard them from future strife. They also moved into the cities, trying to reclaim whatever industrial areas they could.

This proved exceptionally difficult, as the densely packed masses objected to my ancestors' attempts to aid them. Despite the grinding poverty, lack of security and horrid conditions, many people opposed my family out of vile loyalty to either the Republic or House Chauki. Their reticence put the entire planet at risk, as the godless and freethinking ways of the cities threatened to spread to the countryside. It took almost a century to bring the entire planet under control, and the Second Republic loyalists proved almost impossible to wipe out. Even now, rumors of democratic evildoers crop up, especially in Djehut and Ashmunen.

Still, eventually the forces of grace and virtue won out. The democrats tried to force out the Scravers, believing them both in league with us and out to corrupt the cities. The Castenda came to the Scravers' aid, giving them money and succor. The Scravers managed to reinforce their positions in the city and carried out a distasteful (though successful) campaign of assassination and intimidation against the nonbelievers. With their operatives in the cities and our armies without, only right could prevail.

Unfortunately, we have never successfully eliminated all unrighteous thought from this world. Its ancient ties to Sathraists seem to have forever warped it, as has its long adherence to the ways of the Second Republic. Some people have implied that these traits have infected the Hazat here as well, pointing to prominent Sutek Hazat who have gone mad, committed grotesque crimes, or run afoul of the Inquisition.

Such whispers became more intense just before the Emperor Wars and during their earliest days. Beginning the 50th century, our house had suffered innumerable splits and divisions, and the many branches rarely communicated. Part of this stemmed from the abysmal nature of communications at that time, but more had to do with petty hatreds and feuds. Thus when the young Prince Juan Jacobi Nelson Eduardo de Aragon began his drive to reunite us, the rumors became fierce.

Prince Juan's more fervent supporters on Sutek accused the Castendas of idolatry, Antimony and worse. The Castendas called those same supporters brainwashed puppets and democratic sympathizers. When Prince Juan made his call in 4953 for Sutek to provide a one-million soldier levy, the Castendas refused. When many local nobles supported Prince Juan, including my own grandfather, Baron Javier Dilip Kiran Rajeev Hiretia de Calveron, the Castenda moved quickly to bring them into line. My uncle was on his way home from meeting with Baroness Esuala Jahayez Li Halan, then Li Halan ambassador to Sutek, when agents for Duchess Amanda Sorel Victoriana Castenda de Sutek placed him under ducal protection. Grandfather incapacitated more than a dozen of these agents before they successfully put him in their "protection."

Our lands, and those of Prince Juan's other supporters, came under ducal authority. Duchess Amanda asserted not only her freedom from Prince Juan's dictates, but also a claim to leadership of the entire house. She insisted that the Prince relinquish his crown to her. Prince Juan marshaled a fleet at Aragon and prepared to rebut her claim.

My parents told me that the key battle was on the plains of Scarabi, near where Prince Juan landed his force. His initial bombardment and early actions led Duchess Amanda to believe his assault would come near her own castle. She ignored Juan's initial landing at Scarabi, and he quickly reinforced it before anyone realized it was his main thrust. The duchess did prove her strategic ability, however, as she mounted a counteroffensive that almost drove Prince Juan off the planet.

Two elements undermined her counterattack. The first was the prince's determined resistance, lead by not only his most talented nobles, but also by a number of exceptionally motivated commoners. Several names gained fief-wide renown in the battle, including two of today's leading Estancia: Marco Demano and Geraldine Fereel.

The second factor was the Sutek nobility's notorious inability to work together. Duchess Amanda put together an attack force of some of the best warriors on the planet, but found it difficult to get support for them. Many of the nobles on Scarabi supported Prince Juan. Those who did not would lend only token forces to her effort for fear that their neighbors would use this time of weakness to attack them.

After Duchess Amanda's counterattack broke against Prince Juan's forces, she could mount little in the way of effective opposition. Several months later, Baroness Felicity Mar Decados managed to broker a deal to end the fighting. While details of these negotiations remain secret, most of Sutek's lands returned to their pre-hostility ownership, though the planet's leading nobles pledged their allegiance to Prince Juan, and he received grants of land from the duchess and her leading supporters.

The negotiations also had the side effect of bringing my house closer to the Decados. Decados notables began appearing on Sutek with regularity, and for a while Decados fashions became all the rage among our nobility. When we attacked Byzantium Secundus in 4979, their nobles helped us coordinate our attacks. Though I was barely more than a

baby at the time, I remember seeing prominent Decados in the strategy sessions. Since my family has long believed in preparing us for war at a young age, and because my grandfather and parents played notable roles in the planning, I sat under those great tables as master tacticians outlined their strategies. I also met Taretha Juliet Decados for the first time, as her parents also felt that bringing her to these meetings would prove a great beginning for her military training.

Though we failed to hold Byzantium Secundus after our attack, the Decados have maintained their influence on Sutek. While they owned a fair amount of land on the planet before the Emperor Wars, long having a keen interest in the Anunnaki sites, they bought much more. We Hazat still own most of the world, but we (and others) sold and traded a fair amount to the Decados. I've heard it joked that all their plots and schemes on Byzantium Secundus get conceived on Severus, gestate on Sutek and come screaming from the womb on Byzantium Secundus.

Sutek also saw some fighting later in the Emperor Wars. Hawkwood commandos attacked here to disrupt our preparations for the Siege of Jericho. Following that horrific battle, a large Muster force, supported by both Hawkwood and al-Malik forces, landed here to enforce the Emperor's will. After a year of fighting, during which a number of major manufacturing centers fell into ruin, a cease-fire brought us the peace we have today.

Of course, certain elements voiced displeasure over the cease-fire. Following the embarrassment of the failed Siege of Jericho, many military leaders itched for another try at Byzantium Secundus — and at you, my Emperor. Many Sutek nobles objected to this peace forced on them from Aragon, and feared a powerful Imperial force only one jump away (especially since they have always worried about the huge Church military kept one jump away at Holy Terra). They mutinied, and only the skilled diplomacy of Duke Jose Alfonso Louis Eduardo de Aragon (backed, some say, by Dervishes from Vera Cruz), managed to end this rebellion before it could spread. While most of Sutek remains immensely relieved at the end of the Emperor Wars, at least a few people would like to see them restart.

Solar System

All of Sutek's 13 major heavenly bodies have seen some kind of human habitation during the system's 2,500 years of colonization, but most of these sites have worn out their worth and fallen into disuse.

Mercury II: This small planet near Sutek's sun saw construction of a major research center during the First Republic. Revived during the Second Republic, the Fall left it without funds. I know of no visits there within the past 500 years, as the heat and radiation test even the sturdiest space-

craft. I doubt anything still exists there, but one never knows.

Dominey (Ghost, Parish): Heavily populated during the Second Republic, this large world (1.5 times Sutek's mass) still has a substantial population, though its populace must live in insulated cities far beneath the surface. Their mining is responsible for much of the metals and minerals we use on Sutek. Dominey's two moons, Ghost and Parish, each have small populations as well.

Cregstar: While humans managed to colonize this world during the Second Republic, its constant volcanic upheavals have stymied even the best terraformers. Its last citizens died in massive eruptions around 4100. Sutek tried to arrange a rescue, but failed to get there in time.

Sutek (Khonsu, Oculus): This world's similarities to Holy Terra never fail to amaze scholars and mystics alike. The main difference lies in its two moons, Khonsu and Oculus. Khonsu differs little from Holy Terra's moon. Heavily mined and populated during the First Republic, its usefulness declined as its minerals gave out. We maintain a small spaceport there, but most of Khonsu's ancient domed cities are uninhabited. Scravers still find valuable objects there on occasion. Oculus, while much smaller, has more people living on it, as its life support systems make the moon even more habitable than Sutek itself.

Yharit: During the Second Republic, terraformers managed to convert a substantial amount of this windy planet to farming, but this required special crops, fertilizers, and more. After the Fall, many of the farms fell into neglect, and crops either died away or mutated. Now the planet grows little that humans find edible, and plant life dominates those parts of the planet that have not become completely lifeless. The descendants of the ancient farmers have declined as well, and now live an extremely primitive life gathering whatever food they can. A few Hazat have tried to reclaim parts of the planet, with no success. It has great potential, but the Pancreator has apparently decided that Yharit should return to its original form.

Kastaga: This gas giant hosts one of the oddest Anunnaki relics yet discovered: a giant disk floating in its toxic atmosphere. Undiscovered until well into the Second Republic, it lay hidden deep in Kastaga's swirling gases. Almost a kilometer in diameter, this disk, with its odd symbols and even more bizarre light displays, uses no discernible power source to stay afloat. Attempts to move it proved impossible. The Second Republic put a space station in orbit to study the relic, but discovered little before the Fall forced its abandonment. Several hundred years ago, Engineers reported that the space station had fallen from its orbit, and Kastaga's gravity probably destroyed it.

Twenty-Something (Iep, Whever): Named for its many moons (as well as the youth of its discoverer), the giant planet Twenty-Something became a major staging area for Sathraists during their revolt against the First Republic. They tried to create manufacturing centers and living complexes on its two largest moons, Iep and Whever. The First Republic destroyed all trace of these centers, and no further attempts at colonization have succeeded since then. Mining still takes place on Twenty-Something's surface, but these expensive efforts bring forth little to enrich my house.

Exelon: While this planet also attracted numerous Sathraists, it has remained inhabited since the First Republic. Its orbit is almost exactly the same as that of the system's jumpgate, and it has stayed close to it for all 2,500 years humans have been here. Thus Exelon serves as a refueling station, repair spot and agora for those who can't reach Sutek – or who don't want to.

People and Places

A crowded planet, Sutek has almost as many sites of interest as Holy Terra itself. Duchess Elena Cindias Victoriana Castenda de Sutek rules the planet from her spacious palace in ancient Djehut. "Rules" does not accurately reflect her role, however. The Castenda Hazat, who own most of the planet, have rarely agreed on anything, and "riding herd" might better describe what Duchess Elena does. While Sutek's largest landholder, as well as the leading member of its leading family, every decision she makes seems to invite discord.

She took over control of her family's estates when her mother, Duchess Amanda, went into seclusion following that embarrassing incident on Oculus. Not quite the warrior her mother was, Duchess Elena has instead sought success as a diplomat, trying to bring some unity to the Castendas. That she has done so well at this job is testimony both to her own skills and to the assistance of Duchess Salandra Decados, a frequent guest at her estates. Duchess Salandra sometimes seems to be everywhere on Sutek, visiting nobles, taking pilgrimages to ancient Anunnaki sites, and overseeing the growing Decados holdings. Her renowned Oubliette Mind-Physick, Hetairae Pythia, oversees Duchess Amanda's care, though some say a visit from Pythia also preceded that awful incident.

Duchess Elena seems to have made recovering Sutek's lost Anunnaki relics a high priority, and the search for these has consumed many of the planet's nobles. More than a few nobles have tried to pass off old family heirlooms as items of power, only to be embarrassed when they turned out to be nothing of the kind. I feel that many of these people actually believed they had ancient relics, only to discover that legends are not always true. Still, many powerful items have existed on Sutek, so even the oddest legend may well have some truth to it.

For instance, my own family long guarded St. Belchair's scepter. This ancient rod, once owned by Horace the Learned

Man's first student, could reveal proper courses and actions to those who prayed over it. Stories first speak of Belchair wielding this scepter when he and two others ascended Mt. Tetet in search of Anunnaki ruins. It usually rested in our villa near Ptah-Seker, only leaving its protected chest when house leaders called for it. Thus, my amazement knew no limits when rumors spread that my parents had taken it to Hira and lost it in the defense of Fort Omala.

I saw it thrice as a child. The ancient glyphs and designs seemed to leap and play in my vision, making it almost impossible to describe. My third encounter was the most vivid. Two knights, Don Dumuzi Eneki de Huangti and Don Siccaro Petard Castenda, had each offered me a role as his page. I went to pray for guidance over the scepter. Father Restar saw me at my devotions and offered to let me hold the scepter while I prayed. This was the first time the various embellishments on the scepter seemed to make sense to me. For once they did not swim and dart out of my cognizance. I left the chapel still unsure of what to do, but that night my dreams swarmed with dark images of glory and infamy, honor and dishonor. When I awoke, I knew that serving Don Siccaro would leave me covered in glory but with my honor questionable. Being Don Dumuzi's page meant the exact opposite, and his was the service I sought. No matter how difficult the duties became, or how bleak the future, the certainty of my visions calmed my soul in the face of all adversity.

Other relics have similar, and sometimes more spectacular, effects. St. Gloriana's death mask, allegedly formed from prehuman ruins near where humans first landed on Sutek, has been peeled from the faces of people just killed by suffocation. Legends say that it crawls over its victims, moving in and out of their skin and causing them immense pleasure before they die. The Dread Starship, allegedly found in space near Exelon, gives those who touch it such a sense of foreboding that they become afraid to act, move or even think for days at a time. Claims for others include protecting entire planets from disease, keeping their beasts docile or even making the suns shine brighter. One scholar I talked to told me that the relics, like the jumpgates, have purposes we have not even begun to fathom.

Whatever their purpose, they seem to have captured Sutek in a whole new web of excitement. Scravers and Hazat, Eskatonics and hesychasts, and many more recently began tracking down any rumor of an artifact. Thus, my own efforts to recover St. Belchair's scepter lead me all over the planet. I began in Ptah-Seker, the nearest city to my family's historical manor. One of the oldest cities on the planet's main continent, Ptah-Seker sits in the northwest arm of Pleroma, Sutek's dominant land mass. Pleroma covers almost 50 percent of the planet's surface, and humans have lived on it continuously since the First Republic.

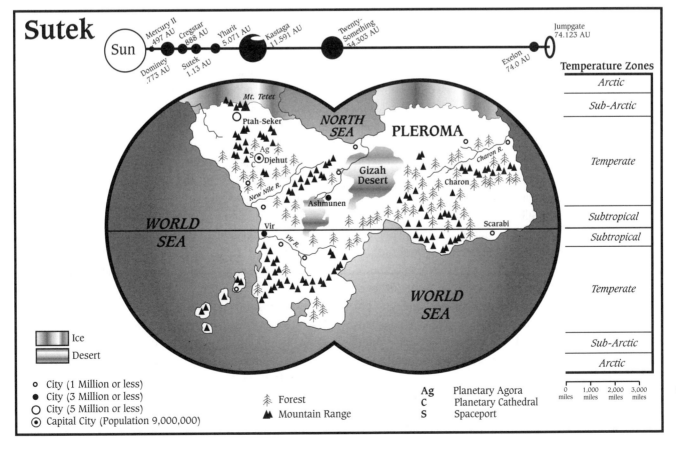

Historians say that the continent has seen extensive changes through the years. Aside from frequent attempts at terraforming, including one by Governor Suchori trying to force a mountain range to spell his name, the mere presence of human habitation has caused many modifications. Priests at St. Esmerelda's once showed me a magic lantern show created by some of Ptah-Seker's ancient founders. I found the fact that some of their structures still stand absolutely amazing. However, much of the show left me feeling odd. Differences as minor as the types of trees growing in the nearby forests, odd animal types I have never seen, and a more vibrant sun all felt alien. Mt. Tetet itself appeared different to me, and its towering peaks lacked the perpetual snow that make it seem both clean and inaccessible.

Apollo's Palace, a museum dedicated to human travel, sits near the outskirts of Ptah-Seker. Its curator, Bing Marcalata, claims to have been on the ship that rediscovered Iver. Since retiring from the spaceways, he devoted his life to keeping the history of space alive, and took over this ramshackle depository. He has added a few interesting items to his collection, such as Diaspora-era ship guns, an early Sathra damper, and part of an Ur-Ukar ship, but he claims more lie buried around Sutek. In fact, he recently began excavations under the museum itself, and who knows what he may find.

While my quest began with my family estates, it quickly took me to Djehut, Sutek's capitol and commercial center. Humans have traded, bartered and sold here for millennia, dating all the way back to the First Republic. During its earliest days, Djehut provided a central meeting place where the planet's independent colonists could show off their wares to zaibatsu buyers and the growing number of free merchants. During the Diaspora, it became one of the most significant trade points in the Known Worlds. With the declining First Republic at odds with almost all the worlds declaring their freedom, Djehut became the primary way for goods to reach the massive markets of Urth. Since Urth's leaders made many of these goods illegal, and even banned Sutek's goods on occasion, my home world began to earn its continued reputation for smuggling.

Djehut's importance declined during the Second Republic as the centers of commerce dispersed throughout the universe, and it has never regained its old place of importance. Even though Sutek's own population rivaled that of many other established worlds, planets like Byzantium Secundus, Criticorum and others rapidly overshadowed it. While many merchants and lawyers made their homes here, most found themselves involved in less important (and less profitable) deals than their colleagues elsewhere.

This remains the case today, though I would not care to argue this point with any denizen of the Djehut agora. The League, all the Royal Houses, and even the Church main-

tain offices here, for much is bought and sold within its walls. The agora itself is really several urban districts, though most people consider them all one and the same. It begins with Terminus spaceport just outside the city and sprawls out to some of Djehut's most (and least) fashionable areas.

When Sutek natives refer to the agora, they usually mean the giant bazaar that covers almost 40 acres on the north side of the city. Here vendors of all types hawk their wares to anyone who wants them. Most of the merchants work out of makeshift stalls, screaming and begging for anyone who passes by to enter. Most of these stalls seem built and placed without rhyme or reason. A holovid dealer might set up shop next to a purveyor of animal foods, trying to be heard over the shouting of the rug seller across the way. While some stores are permanent structures, most merchants throw up a building one day, putting it wherever they can find space, and tear it down once they sell all their goods. Ale, clothes, tools, teas, bibles, weapons and more are all sold here.

Guilds doing the most business with the spaceport own or rent buildings just outside Terminus. The Scravers have the most obvious presence here, with their Landsky geodesic dome. Their guild gained prominence on Sutek early, salvaging the many remnants of previous societies, and using the proceeds from these operations to start others. They claim that their ancestors rebuilt Terminus during the Diaspora, and use this claim (as well as the strength of their service sectors) to justify their dominance in Djehut's agora.

Circling this bazaar, but concentrated to its east, are the many guild centers of the agora. Here the guilds train new workers, hold their many meetings, and cut the deals too big or too sensitive to handle in the bazaar. While many high-ranking nobles would never think of shopping in the bazaar, preferring to send servants to run their errands, all love to shop in the guild centers. The arrival of a De Vatha cargo ship from Byzantium Secundus can bring hundreds with wallet in hand. The centers are where one goes for the best jewelry, fine wines, and sophisticated think machines.

On the edge of the city, between the guild centers and Terminus spaceport, are giant marshalling yards for livestock and other living creatures that might pass through Djehut. Other natural resources also come through the marshalling yard before making their way to their final destinations. Here spaceship captains arrange for the loading of large cargoes and merchants come shopping for new goods. The Scravers definitely run things here, and all the drivers, stewards and bearers work for them.

I met with Boss Vasquel Agustin at the Landsky Dome in order to track down rumors of St. Belchair's scepter. My family has sought him out whenever we have need of specialized information, and he did not let me down. Thus, my quest took me back to the heart of Ptah-Seker — the oldest

parts of the city.

Some have likened Ptah-Seker to a Decados noble applying makeup, adding layer upon layer and hoping that it will eventually look good. As with most of Sutek, many groups own land in the city, and each has its own idea of how things should look. The city's outermost districts have the most recent and (in my opinion) most attractive buildings. Venturing further into the city, the signs of age and decay grew. On the outskirts, builders turned freshly carved stone and newly painted wood into unique dwellings and shops designed as much for beauty as utility. Buildings constructed in earlier times show both their age and their purpose, but less of the decoration of today's.

Conversations with relic dealers finally led me to the very oldest part of the city, also known as Salchicha, for the meaty smell that seems to permeate everything. Here a small community all its own exists, with self-styled nobles (albeit clad in rags), their hulking goons, and their serfs, who farm crops grown in filth and muck. Word had reached me of a bizarre sect of St. Belchair worshippers, and I sought them out for what they might know.

I found one, and under the threat of violence, he told me where the rest met. A passageway through abandoned sewers seemed an odd path to a worship service, so after ensuring that the worshipper I found would not warn his friends (he eventually recovered from this), I armed myself and prepared to join in their devotions. The path through the sewers began in new stone construction but soon lead to maxicrete and even more ancient parts.

To my amazement, their sanctuary turned out to be the hull of an ancient space freighter, no doubt abandoned millennia ago. Its key defenses proved to be two golems who once served passengers on the ship, as well as a number of devious traps they had scattered around the spaceship. While discoveries like an ancient freighter are not unheard of, and Scravers still search this world for such junk, this one shone despite the centuries of dirt and filth. That it could have remained hidden in the heart of Ptah-Seker for so long was even more amazing. Most amazing was the purpose for which they used this hull — to conduct Antimonistic rites to the demons between the stars.

It seems they believed St. Belchair had used his fabled scepter to trap a four-headed demon lord in the depths of Mt. Tetet. They hoped to free this creature by getting the scepter off planet. Before Inquisitors could arrive to cart off what was left of the cultists, one admitted that they had stolen the scepter from my family's villa. The Inquisitors held on to it for several years before a noble offered to take it with him to Aragon.

With at least a general idea of who had taken the scepter, and bolstered by the knowledge that my parents had not been the ones to remove it from Sutek, I made my way to the spaceport at Djehut to continue my travels. I went by rail, still the easiest way to traverse the planet, and spent as much time contemplating the worn crop fields, the faded buildings and the tired peasants as I did the task before me.

Djehut remained much as it has been for hundreds of years — cramped, dirty and constantly eventful. Packed with industry, nobles and guilds have long made money here while priests have made sermons. The spaceport was like a microcosm of the entire city, with ancient buildings fulfilling the same roles they did during the First Republic. The first ship leaving for Aragon proved to be a Scraver gambling liner, and as I left Sutek I could only ponder the great gamble that once took humanity to the stars, and wonder whether winning that bet actually paid off.

Aragon

We Hazat have long pointed with pride at the beauty that is Aragon. To those who deride us as loving nothing but war, we point to the awe-inspiring glory of Castle Furias. To those who say destruction is our highest aspiration, we display the massive factories of Zamora and their nonstop flow of products. To those who claim we love nothing but killing, we show Aragon's pastoral fields and the happy peasants of Quechua. Aragon has all the splendor any world could want — and more than a few of the problems.

History

The first humans to visit Aragon back in 2413 came from Vera Cruz, and they carried with them that world's agrarian focus. The agrogiant TDA found expanding to new worlds extremely profitable. It could sell its immense holdings on Urth for huge sums and begin whole new operations on new planets for next to nothing. These new operations attracted customers for their "exotic alien delicacies" and avoided scrutiny for their experimental foods and harsh worker treatment. Still, TDA had no shortage of workers begging to leave their overcrowded homeworld, and the company's security force set about making Vera Cruz and Aragon safe from native threats and (more importantly) other zaibatsu.

TDA filled both planets quickly, focusing on the most promising farmland. Other zaibatsu also sought out these

Aragon Traits

Cathedral: Saint Emanuel Cathedral (Orthodox)

Agora: Port Isabella (Charioteer)

Garrison: 7

Capital: Castle Furias (in Bermeja)

Jumps: 1

Adjacent Worlds: Byzantium Secundus, Leagueheim (nightside), Vera Cruz (nightside)

Solar System: Hermes (.374 AU), Aragon (.989 AU), Teruel (1.373 AU), Jalapa (3.410), Alvarado (6.845), Jumpgate (57 AU)

Tech: 5

Human Population: 1.16 billion

Alien Population: 50,000 (mainly Ur-Obun and Etyri)

Resources: Energy, trace minerals

Exports: Industrial furnaces, dynamos, machinery, tools, vehicles, industrial goods, manufacturing equipment, weapons

Landscape: The temperate continent of Quecha is free of intense weather, though the other continents are not so lucky. Despite the fading suns phenomenon, Aragon is a relatively warm world.

worlds, however, and conflicts broke out constantly. Alliances and enmities shifted almost daily during the First Republic. Where economic interests did not conflict, TDA worked well with other corporations. For instance, two energy companies constantly battled over giant oil fields in the Quechua desert and the Disinean Sea. TDA would side with one and then the other based on their needs that day, since it could do little farming in their battle zones. On the other hand, when TDA's own needs came into conflict with someone else's, the zaibatsu proved a fierce opponent.

When the massive Kanawha mining consortium created a complex in Quechua, they also claimed control over much of Aragon's fresh water. Instead of paying the fees required to establish desalinization operations, TDA decided to unleash the full might of its security forces. TDA's hope was to both reclaim the water and create an object lesson for anyone else who might move in on its territory.

Henri Assat, TDA's vice president for Aragon, took a personal interest in the new competitor. TDA's security forces began raiding Kanawha's facilities around the planet. These hit-and-run attacks disrupted some mining operations, but technicians quickly brought operations back on line, and Kanawha began shipping in the latest golem defensive systems. TDA's security forces began taking heavy casualties in every raid, and the home office let Assat know that such a waste of resources would not be permitted. Instead, Kanawha began sending mercenaries against TDA. Since

agriculture was even more labor intensive than mining, and TDA's workers less protected than Kanawha's, the casualties inflicted on the farmers put all its operations at risk.

In order to stem the losses, Assat offered the workers money, land and weapons to fight Kanawha. When the mercenaries began encountering armed opposition on every attack, they changed their tactics, avoided combat and waited for their contracts to run out. When they left, the farmers began targeting their anger at TDA's operations, and the combination of renewed security force raids, worker attacks and the decline of the First Republic finally crippled Kanawha.

Assat's compromise made a number of the planet's workers rich, with their own land and operations. When Kanawha's Aragon operations declined, these workers took over much of its land and equipment. When the Sathra revolt began a generation later, they were well positioned to challenge TDA for dominance on the planet. The Chaukis, the most successful of these families, soon took the lead, and began seizing TDA land "for the good of the people."

TDA had hoped to counteract the farmers' growing influence by shipping in even more workers from Urth, but these had no loyalty to the zaibatsu. The Chaukis already had ties to TDA's security forces, and bribed these troops to their side. With neither its own security forces or the First Republic's able to enforce its claims, TDA opted for an army of mercenaries to enforce its will.

As the Sathra revolt wound down, large numbers of experienced troops found themselves without work. TDA hired droves of these, and they fell on Aragon in a frenzy of destruction. The Chaukis had many weapons remaining from previous battles on the planet (Kanawha was not the only zaibatsu with which TDA had feuded), but lacked the manpower to drive off the invaders. Despite the trying circumstances under which most of TDA's workers lived, they did not rally to the Chauki banner, seeing little reason to hope it would prove better than the zaibatsu.

The war seesawed back and forth, with neither side able to gain the upper hand. Chauki forces also suffered defeats on Vera Cruz, and soon only the Aragon workers offered them any hope. Efforts to galvanize this force proved fruitless until the Chaukis brought in Clarrisa Trumon, a noted promoter of her day. Trumon had already helped establish House Alecto, and she convinced the Chauki's to announce their own noble lineage. It did not hurt that they claimed to be descended from the ancient kings who once ruled in the southern part of Urth's western hemisphere — also the home of a majority of TDA's workers.

Capitalizing on this announcement (and blanketing the planet with "evidence" of TDA's brutalities), the new House Chauki finally began generating recruits. The experienced soldiers of the security forces trained these legions, and within a year the tide had shifted in their favor. TDA's for-

tunes also suffered on other worlds, and as the First Republic declined, the zaibatsu found its earlier decision to abandon Urth more and more of a hindrance, as claims to its land elsewhere spread.

When House Chauki finally won on Aragon, TDA was but a shell of its former self. House Chauki claimed Aragon and Vera Cruz at this time, and set about consolidating its rule. This began a land rush on both of these planets, as numerous groups tried to seize TDA's abandoned holdings. House Chauki ended up with a majority of its land, but they could not get it all. Other groups took prime estates, and many followed the Chauki lead of declaring themselves noble houses.

House Chauki first tried to establish a new republic centered on Aragon, but quickly gave up in the face of hostility on other planets and increased competition at home. Various groups tried to claim its land, and the Chaukis found themselves beset on many sides. When diplomacy failed, as it often did with the Chaukis, they turned to the descendants of Emanuel Primitivo Hazat, once head of TDA's security forces.

His scion now served as House Chauki's hereditary defenders, and had taken his name to honor his accomplishments in helping topple the ungodly First Republic. This force helped stabilize noble rule on the planet, proving especially competent at stopping the occasional peasant rebellions that Chauki misrule provoked. To minimize this threat, the Hazat took more and more of the onus of security upon itself, freeing the peasants from the temptation of armed revolt. The Hazat also lead efforts to spread Chauki rule to other worlds, especially Sutek and Hira (see Vera Cruz, below). We even tried to bring Holy Terra under our protection, but the rising power of the Church lessened the need for that.

Thus, after establishing a noble house that should have proved a force for prudence and solidity for ages, we watched in amazement as the Chaukis tried to throw away all we had established. During the last years of the Diaspora, numerous merchant conglomerates began rising again, much as they had during the First Republic. Centered on Byzantium Secundus, but with their tentacles reaching everywhere, these new zaibatsu gained more power than most planetary rulers.

My ancestors watched with horror as House Chauki become more entangled with the growing merchant class. Perhaps it was Aragon's proximity to Byzantium Secundus, or maybe the Chaukis had suffered from democratic leanings all along, but the house supported efforts to establish the Second Republic. Their worlds became bulwarks for this evil, and House Chauki profited from the tremendous flow of wealth streaming to Byzantium Secundus. In fact, some Chaukis' even gave up their noble titles, preferring to promote "equality and fraternity" with the peasantry.

Of course, the evil of the Second Republic could not last. Despite the many technological wonders sprouting like weeds on Aragon and other worlds, discontent began to spread. Despite all the claims of "perpetual peace," we Hazat maintained our military, knowing it would one day be needed. Then, in 3977, House Chauki called for us to disarm. It claimed the Second Republic provided all the protection anyone needed, and that other armed groups "promoted instability." We, whose weapons had proved instrumental in establishing the Chaukis' power, would promote instability!

Tensions between the Hazat and House Chauki grew rapidly, and several individual Hazat outposts came under attack from Second Republic police, who claimed their inhabitants were fomenting armed insurrection. Then General Emanuel Huevo Iman discovered that Chauki leaders had tried to conceal our own descent from Urth nobility, fearing that the people would flock to our real heritage instead of their contrived background. This sin, coupled with the many crimes House Chauki was then perpetrating upon its people, forced our hand.

Their actions offended more than just us. Houses Li Halan and House Merovia (lost since the Fall) both loaned us spaceships and offered troops for our cause. House Decados joined them on Byzantium Secundus to argue our case, thus keeping the Second Republic from unleashing the bulk of its forces against us. Some say the Patriarch himself helped us, and I believe the Church saw the rightness of our actions.

The early fights took the form of probing attacks and attempts to consolidate our positions. While we controlled much of the Chaukis' military might, their technicians prevented us from broadcasting our righteous message to the peasantry. They bombarded the populace with slanderous propaganda and turned many people against us. Cities that should have welcomed our liberating forces violently opposed us, leading to their own destruction.

The conflict on Byzantium Secundus proved just as bitter (and just as important) as that on Aragon. The Chaukis desperately tried to get the Second Republic to intervene. We rightly pointed to legal doctrines prohibiting such actions. Early in the formation of the Second Republic, a number of worlds agreed to join only if they could continue to decide their own political fate. This lead to the doctrine of planets' rights, aimed at keeping the Republic out of internal political matters.

The Chaukis argued that this rule of law did not apply to what they called an armed coup d'état, and that they, as the hereditary rulers of Aragon, Vera Cruz and other worlds, could call for such intervention. They also tricked local governing bodies on these worlds to call for Second Republic help, but together with our allies we managed to prevent this. While the Chaukis schemed and plotted, our friends valiantly derailed their efforts to summon off-world help. We held up debate in the Republican Council, got legal injunctions issued against efforts to send reinforcements and convinced other planets to put an arms embargo on Chauki worlds. Since we already had all the weapons we needed, this did not hurt us. Finally, our own new designation as a noble house gained us sympathy from those other nobles who believed the Second Republic had no right to dictate to them.

Our best efforts could not prevent deluded adventurers from around the Republic from trying to help the Chauki. Several legions of these reached our worlds, and many more sent money and equipment to help the Chauki cause. These legions, combined with the many peasants the Chaukis' enlisted to fight their battles, proved more effective than we expected. Not all modern Hazat have learned the lessons of overconfidence we displayed during this time, but it is a lesson all should heed. Those Hazat who believed our trained military would roll over House Chauki's novice soldiers received a rude awakening.

Inspired by the Chaukis' lies and deceptions, this hastily constructed army proved surprisingly potent, and took every opportunity to exploit its advantages. Early on, House Chauki controlled the cities, and dislodging the nobles from these urban killing zones proved next to impossible. When House Chauki did fight in rural areas, it was in places its troops knew well, and they proved extremely difficult to dislodge. They also carried out the worst kind of guerilla warfare, sending squads on suicide missions against our weakest positions. They raided our supply bases, attacked troop convoys, and sabotaged our communication arrays. They also spread their foul propaganda into our regions, trying to turn our own followers against us.

Their greatest advantage, however, came in their mastery of the most repulsive forms of technology. Not only could they continue to bombard us with the most noxious lies, but also they could disrupt our own communications with ease. Their loathsome think machine freaks barred our access to the intraplanetary networks, tied up our finances, interfered with our allies' activities, disrupted our intelligence gathering and even hurt such critical activities as spaceship landings.

Thus, they thwarted our efforts to bring about a quick and peaceful transfer of power. Instead, the conflict became a long and bloody struggle, and we suffered unwarranted casualties. The Pancreator protected us during these dark times, however, and blessed us with the inspired leadership of Saint Emanuel. He succeeded in bringing the Chaukis' loathsome use of technology to the Church's attention, and the Church's own think machine warriors began to help us. He also made other groups aware of House Chauki's base nature and pernicious activities, and these groups took ac-

tions of their own. Chaukis began dying across the Republic.

The Chauki strongholds on Aragon began to suffer, and our successes on planet grew much like our successes off planet. Slowly we forced them back, until only Bermeja remained theirs. No victory could be complete without this central city, and we redoubled our efforts to liberate it. Our hover tanks soared around the city on an hourly basis, and our artillery began around the clock efforts to destroy Chauki barriers, but still the Chaukis and their brainwashed followers held on. We attacked it from orbit, stormed its walls, and blocked off all food and supplies, but still it held out. We did not liberate it until we had killed almost everyone within.

The remaining Chaukis finally managed to turn the Republic against us despite the rightness of our cause. They charged us with genocide, revolution, conspiracy and more. They claimed that nothing more than greed and a lust for power inspired our duty. Following a Church visit to Bermeja, new rumors spread that the only reason the Church had sided with us was to obtain five Anunnaki relics in the city, relics that the Church suddenly believed to be of great power. I think the fact that only one of these relics has shown up since disproves such a theory.

The Second Republic began preparations to move against us, but then its own sins caught up with it. Its own Fall from its heights of arrogance stopped both its aggression against us and Chauki hopes of regaining the house's possessions. We moved as quickly as possible to consolidate our gains on Aragon, and while other factions also seized some land, we managed to bring the bulk of the planet under our benevolent leadership.

For the next several hundred years, unfortunately, Aragon saw regular conflict. We battled upstart houses wanting our land, corporations left over from the Second Republic, desert nomads, and finally barbarian raiders. After Vladimir's unfortunate death, we found ourselves having to battle other major houses, and managed to extend our rulership of Aragon through battles with the Alectos and the Windsors. However, this constant warfare prevented us from providing for our serfs as we wanted, and also destroyed much of the planet's infrastructure. Feuds between different lines within the house also disrupted attempts to better the planet, and alliances had fractured appallingly by the time of Prince Juan's father, Prince Giallo Rolus Jahasta Matingo Eduardo de Aragon (also known as "The Gold Mantis"). The Justus line ruled much of the planet, but showed little interest in leading it.

Prince Giallo began the long process of reunifying the world, and it took him most of the 115 years of his life. After his death in battle at Fortress Concordita, Prince Juan took over and completed the process. While Aragon did not suffer as much during the Emperor Wars as did Sutek, it did

see its share of fighting. Hawkwood, al-Malik and Li Halan troops all landed on the planet at one time or another, but we had little difficulty driving them off.

Now Aragon has a chance to enter a golden age of peace, prosperity and moral fitness. Not only is the entire world under the gracious leadership of Prince Juan, but the Church has also expanded its missions. While the military still calls many of my brothers and sisters, more than a few joined the Church, and they spread the Prophet's words to every fief and field.

Solar System

My father once described the heavens of Aragon as tiny jewels wrapped around a scintillating ruby, and I can only agree with him. Aragon's beautiful red star, while affected by the fading suns phenomenon, still shines beautifully, and each planet in orbit around it glitters and gleams in its light.

Hermes: Little more than a dot in sky, this world glows with heat. Few other heavenly bodies face the sheer heat this planet does, and it can be seen from Aragon all summer long. The Second Republic conducted some research here, and recovered records show that Hermes caught the interest of many corporations, but the Fall precluded whatever investigations they intended.

Aragon (Castile): Beautiful Aragon looks like a multi-hued ball from space, and the lush clouds that float through its sky give it a marbled appearance. Castile, also known as the "red moon" for the great iron deposits visible from orbit, has hosted large mining operations ever since the Diaspora. Castile supplies the raw materials from which Aragon's industry has grown.

Teruel: Extensive terraforming during the Second Republic made this small planet rather habitable, and we still maintain successful fiefs here. Water supply remains this world's primary weakness, and its occasional green forests stand out in stark contrast to the brown and yellow of its earth. Less than 100,000 people currently live here.

Jalapa (Smither, Lost Sign, Ebola): Despite Jalapa's distance from the sun, liquid exists in extensive quantities, warmed both by the planet's own internal heat and the atmosphere's extreme pressure. This is not water, however. Melted metals and combinations of other elements create Jalapa's swirling, ever-changing kaleidoscope of colors. During the Diaspora, explorers discovered some intriguing mixtures in these liquids, and put them to use in a variety of products and medicines. This declined during the Second Republic, but we restarted these operations during the Emperor Wars. While these operations recently encountered difficulties, some Hazat have proposed expanding our extractions. They believe we might find an array of new chemicals.

Alvarado (Crane, Everlost): This gas giant is relatively uninteresting, but its moons have their own attraction. Crane's brilliant white sheen comes from the frozen ammonia covering its surface. Everlost, on the other hand, lies hidden under its own black clouds, a dark diamond concealed in space. Its darkness comes from the heavy metals that have made their way into its atmosphere, and as recently as the Emperor Wars smugglers had set up a base for bringing proscribed goods to Aragon.

People and Places

An arrival on Aragon highlights all the best aspects of Hazat rule. After a brief layover on Byzantium Secundus, my Scraver liner spiraled down through Aragon's peaceful cloud cover and toward the abundant green of western Quechua. Princess Isabella spaceport hummed with activity, and serfs, freemen and guildsmen happily worked side by side loading industrial wares onto ships and unloading foodstuffs, fuels and innumerable other goods. The port gently guided us to our landing, where an honor guard in full dress regalia met our ship. Several prominent nobles and guildsmen inspected the troops, though I noted that none of the Church elders who I saw on the flight joined us. I believe they may have left the gambling liner by some other means than the front door.

The warden of the port, Baroness Filenia Perry Dulcinea de Isabella, offered me the distinct honor of personally reviewing and addressing her troops. This distinction pleased me for many reasons, not the least being its marked contrast to the last time I landed on Aragon. Back then, as a knight fresh in your service as well as one of the few Hazat among the Questing Knights, port guards — less formally dressed and more heavily armed — greeted me. Remembering your admonition to avoid all unnecessary conflict, I ignored their constant insults and attempts at intimidation, no matter how hotly my cheeks burned. I can only hope that my restraint then helped encourage this new hospitality.

The other reason I found addressing the troops so satisfying was that afterward I encountered Manuel Cazrop. Manuel first served with me during the Siege of Jericho, where he helped me rescue what few survivors we could from that horrible incident. Now a master sergeant with Baroness Filenia's forces, Manuel told me that while his previous association with me once hindered his career, now it proved a blessing. Friends I made during the Emperor Wars heard how well he served me, and his career seemed to blossom as word of my new quests spread. Baroness Filenia also took time from her busy schedule to greet me, apologized for the unpleasantness during my last visit, and kindly consented to let Manuel accompany me on my travels across Aragon.

Both Baroness Filenia and I attended my house's great military academy here on Aragon, and that tie helped smooth

things over. She and I spent part of our time together discussing old classmates, toasting both those who achieved prominence and those who never returned home from the wars. While few Hazat complete the entire four-year program the academy recommends, many members of my house attend at least a few classes.

This has made the environs around the academy one of the most interesting urban areas I have ever encountered. Nobles at school have money to spend, but little time to do so. Consequently, they may move into a fine dwelling, but never get around to hiring a housekeeper for it. They may even forget to clean up bloodstains from a duel. They also attract bizarre entourages of young Aragonians, and the academy community boasts a mix of warriors, scholars, philosophers, prostitutes, layabouts, scoundrels and rogues of all types. While not nearly as deadly as other parts of Aragon, it is certainly one of the most treacherous.

My entourage and I began our excursion with the required visits to the planet's leading nobles. While Aragon's social whirl is not the equivalent of Byzantium Secundus', one can easily become lost in it. Most of it is centered on the western end of the Quechan continent, with its heart at Castle Furias. The area around the palace might not be as beautiful as the castle itself, but it has its own unique attractions. Numerous theaters, museums, cathedrals, fine villas and the like fill the lands closest to Castle Furias. Some of the prettiest areas surround the Tassera Gardens. These gardens, begun during the Second Republic and continued until this very day, boast flowers from around the Known Worlds, and feature many whose origins we can only guess.

An even more interesting spot sits behind the gardens, along a bluff by the Athos Canal. Here, in a pretty grove known as the Athos Gardens, roses and violets fill the breeze with their lovely perfume. Shade from Grail magnolia trees and Terran poplars cools its air on even the hottest days, and the clash of Leagueheim steel against ancient swords rings out with amazing regularity.

The Athos Gardens have probably seen more duels than any spot in the Known Worlds. For hundreds of years, members of my house have come here to settle affairs of honor, justice, and testosterone. Such illustrious family members as Don Carlo Jacquile Roma de Setanian, Baronet Mehiel Jeremiah Ristalato Rolas and Baroness Lucinda Dulcinea all found themselves drawing blades here. Not only Hazat come here, however. Duelists from Byzantium Secundus, Leagueheim and more distant places visit the gardens to settle old concerns and test their mettle.

While some joke that the reason the gardens' plants grow so well is due to the huge amount of blood soaked into its soil, my house maintains these grounds for a reason. By having one set place where such potentially deadly contests take place, we can ensure that they end as calmly as pos-

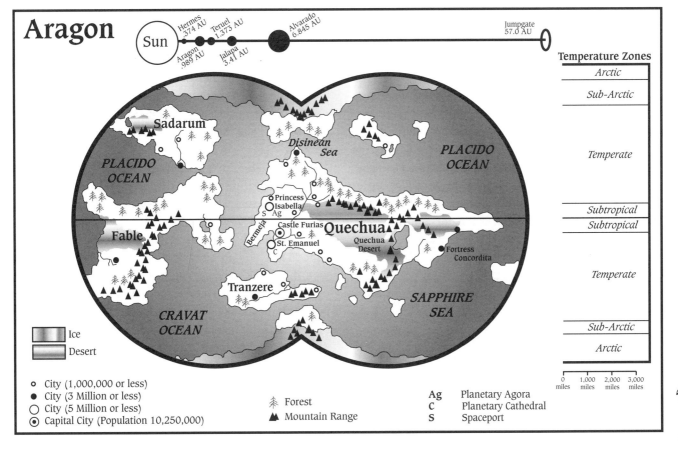

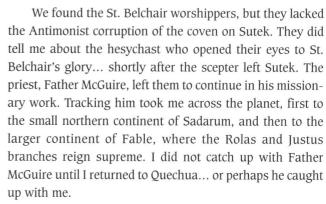

sible. In addition, we can oversee our nobles' development, and help them improve their abilities. Moreover, we do believe dueling builds stronger leaders, for one who has faced death squarely in the face loses some fear of dying but gains a respect for it. She is less likely to throw others' lives away cavalierly, and is more likely to pay what costs are required for success. Finally, we like it, and this is a wonderful place to watch (or fight) a duel.

Of course, the gardens' sublime beauty pales in comparison to Castle Furias itself. Here Prince Juan and his lovely wife, Martia Celestra Justus de Aragon, host beautiful balls and grand soirees. Such events always seem to have a greater exuberance about them when held at Castle Furias, and more than one guest has attributed this to St. Bernado's Globe, an ancient relic said to inspire true passion in people. Sister Halva Lorlia, the cohort I took with me on my journey, noted how the entire castle seemed to sparkle, and how the light always seems to illuminate people and objects in the best way possible. The art that fills the castle appears especially glorious, and artists have told me that works created and displayed here are transcendent.

Prince Juan and Princess Martia greeted me warmly, but the person I most wanted to meet was Don Alfonso Rendell Rolas. Once Prince Juan's security chief, he lost that post at the end of the Emperor Wars when others claimed that our losses stemmed from our spies' failures. Don Alfonso's claims that his orders forced him to make his agents subservient to Decados commands went unheeded, and Baronet Devastio Perata Eduardo de Florencia now oversees our house's security. Still, Don Alfonso learns much of what occurs on Aragon, and he told me about a small circle of St. Belchair worshippers on the east coast of Quechua.

The Justus branch of my family owns much of the eastern part of this continent, and I visited Duchess Karmena Willow Gurthon Justus de Quechua on her lavish estates near the Sapphire Sea. We traveled by flitter over the Quechua desert, where communities and mining operations appear almost randomly. Desert nomads have begun raiding settlements again, but only when they are not battling each other. The nomads had been in decline before the Emperor Wars, but Duchess Karmena says that their ranks have recently swelled with returned veterans and escaped serfs. Her own serfs appeared happy, however, and her lands rich and peaceful. The further I traveled from the heart of her holdings, however, the less content they seemed.

The outer areas still feel the casualties we suffered during the Emperor Wars, and some residents complained (to Miguel, not to me) that little had been done to assist their ravaged work force. Taxes and other burdens remain the same, but fewer hands help with the effort. This discontent has attracted more than a few hesychast priests, and their wild preaching amazed Sister Halva.

We found the St. Belchair worshippers, but they lacked the Antimonist corruption of the coven on Sutek. They did tell me about the hesychast who opened their eyes to St. Belchair's glory… shortly after the scepter left Sutek. The priest, Father McGuire, left them to continue in his missionary work. Tracking him took me across the planet, first to the small northern continent of Sadarum, and then to the larger continent of Fable, where the Rolas and Justus branches reign supreme. I did not catch up with Father McGuire until I returned to Quechua… or perhaps he caught up with me.

Word that two Questing Knights sought him (for Lady Atricia had just joined me) must have reached his ears, and the ambush he set for me almost proved my end. We finally found him in the Bermeja barrio, a part of the giant city I barely even knew existed and had never before seen. The structures varied between ancient towers, often gutted and open to the elements, and recently constructed huts and hovels. Its inhabitants appeared either sullen or violent, and I broke up three fights within two hours. All of the fights involved weapons, and one had already proven deadly before I interrupted it. I have since been told that some of my house's most accomplished soldiers have risen from this barrio, but I find it an unfit training ground.

Father McGuire's residence sat near the center of the barrio, and we saw little outside of it to cause concern. Once a church, it appeared to have become a factory during the Second Republic, but time and vandals had reduced it to the point where we could see only the faintest traces of its history. We entered carefully and quietly, only to discover a horde of barrio residents with no interest in being either careful or quiet. Rather than staying to defeat them, we plunged deeper into the former church, which may well have been McGuire's plan. In its deepest depths, with an armed mob on our tails, we encountered Father McGuire and his acolytes.

Sister Halva says his powers resembled theurgy, but they reeked of Antimony to me. Father McGuire seemed to swell and expand with every dark prayer he uttered, and I found myself slowed and weakened as unseen hands seemed to batter me. The room itself appeared to be some sort of dark chapel, and an army of burning candles filled the air with their rank odor. As the unseen hands threatened to overwhelm us, Miguel left the room, only to return moments later with the mob hot on his heels. I steeled myself to give the best account that I could, for Miguel's taunting had enraged them all the more. However, his desperate tactics did the job for us. The mob dismantled the room in its haste to get at us. It also provided a necessary distraction for Father McGuire, who shifted his attention to deal with his own allies.

We took advantage of this momentary respite to charge

him, and despite his acolytes' martial proficiency, we managed to subdue both them and the heretical father. Sister Halvah provided the finishing blow, striking him down with one of his own candelabras after my own blaster bolt shorted out his shield. The mob dispersed with him unconscious, and a few well-placed shots hurried them along. Before turning Father McGuire over to Church officials at Saint Emanuel, we managed to determine that he never met the noble who supplied him with the scepter. Indeed, the heretical priest managed to hold onto it for several years before the noble arranged to transport it off Aragon. Father McGuire turned

it over to a warrior serving as the noble's agent. His description left us with little doubt that the warrior could only be Rucka Jamon de Luista, a hero of the Emperor Wars who retired to Vera Cruz.

I have since heard that Father McGuire lost his life trying to escape from an Avestite compound in the Quechua desert. I take no pleasure in this knowledge, nor in the injuries I caused his followers. This world has suffered enough. While Aragon still offers unparalleled beauty, the Emperor Wars left deep scars that will take at least a generation to heal.

Vera Cruz

Unlike Aragon, Vera Cruz strikes most as a world of peace and tranquility. The Emperor Wars barely touched this planet. However, Vera Cruz's peaceful present belies its wartorn past. It has paid in blood for the calm it enjoys today. From its origins darkened with Sathraists and other dissident groups, to its feuding owners during the Diaspora, to our liberation of it from the Chaukis, to the Kurgan spies still found there today, strife has never been far from its glistening shores.

History

TDA did not discover Vera Cruz, but it moved on the planet as quickly as if it had. The soil and weather proved perfect for growing crops from Urth, and many of its native plants proved both edible and popular. Only one problem blocked TDA's rapid acquisition of Vera Cruz's land — the original settlers.

Sathraists from Urth's western hemisphere first discovered the planet, and they opened it up to colonization by a number of disenchanted groups from the mother world. These included political refugees, workers dissatisfied with zaibatsu employment, and urbanites fleeing overcrowded slums. TDA always tried to settle planets with its own workers, but this time difficulties became apparent immediately.

First, other groups had already settled the planet's prime arable land, and they showed no interest in moving. Second, when TDA established work camps near the existing communities, it found that its own employees often defected to the other groups. Attempts to force the settlers from their lands with force proved ineffective. Not only had the settlers brought their own weapons with them, but they also still had friendly connections on Urth. As soon as TDA moved against the settlers, word would go out. Boycotts were declared, powerful politicians found themselves forced to act,

and, most importantly, TDA's enemies took advantage of the situation to disrupt the zaibatsu's other operations.

Unlike TDA's Aragon executives, those on Vera Cruz had no interest in pursuing a military solution under such conditions. They changed tact almost at once, insisting that their actions had been misconstrued; they were only seeking to protect other communities when their armed commando teams went storming in. They also sought to make amends, offering substantial amounts of consumer goods in compensation. The executives further promised to make their own operations friendlier to local cultures, and began hiring from the same areas of Urth from which the existing ones came. They encouraged these new employees to form social organizations with locals, and these clubs received funding and facilities from the zaibatsu.

Thus the executives began a more covert method of subverting the existing inhabitants. Vera Cruz's original colonists had created a vibrant, unique mix of social systems, each with its own philosophy, goals, strengths and weaknesses. The generations that followed continued this, though contact between their communities began to lead to a more homogeneous culture. TDA's involvement, however, massively accelerated this process.

As part of its remuneration for the damages it caused, TDA provided massive quantities of consumer goods from Urth, including entertainment programming, educational materials, medical supplies (especially pain killers) and more labor-saving devices. Of course, most of these required replacements fairly soon, and an appeased populace began buying them in large amounts. TDA executives also took care to introduce only those products that would promote values they liked — docility, meekness and materialism.

TDA also did its best to ensure that Vera Cruz's citizens lacked the funds to acquire these goods from other sources,

Vera Cruz Traits

Cathedral: Orthodox

Agora: Charioteer

Garrison: 6

Capital: Los Aztecha

Jumps: 2

Adjacent Worlds: Sutek (dayside), Aragon (dayside), Hira (nightside)

Solar System: Puebla (.94 AU), Vera Cruz (1.3 AU), Albemarle (1.9 AU), Pharis (15.3 AU), Katara (36.1 AU), Jumpgate (37.1 AU)

Tech: 5

Human Population: 750,000,000

Alien Population: 8,000

Resources: Foodstuffs, agricultural goods, consumer goods

Exports: Grain, wheat, corn, furniture, plastics, farming implements, household items

Landscape: Vera Cruz has plenty of jungle, both around the equator and south of it. Much of this is as dark and impenetrable as the day humans discovered this world. The northern areas are more mountainous, with large wooded areas between the mountains and the jungles. Oceans cover less than half of the world.

and soon they began flocking to the better-paying TDA jobs. Once part of the TDA work force, the zaibatsu could instill its values however it desired. Workers thus indoctrinated spread their beliefs to their old homes, and in less than a generation resistance to TDA had become a thing of the past in all but the most remote locales.

TDA could have benefited dramatically from these changes had it not been for the Sathra rebellion. Before the agrogiant could completely exploit Vera Cruz's resources, interstellar trade fell apart. While no longer a Sathraist haven, Vera Cruz still had pockets of such sympathy. Several small dogfights took place in the solar system, and the First Republic sent troops to round up suspected sympathizers on the planet's surface, but the immediate impact on the planet was slight.

The rebellion did stop the constant flow of corporate programming and money to fund TDA's activities. Workers, now accustomed to an unending supply of luxuries, immediately blamed TDA for all their problems. The docile labor force rapidly turned ugly, maddened by the absence of their favorite "Goodbye Kitten" and "Amigos" holovids. One social organization took advantage of this anger — the one that would become the Chaukis.

The Chaukis originally arrived on Vera Cruz in the 24th century as refugees from a failed rebellion in the southern

part of Urth's western hemisphere. This revolt against the power of the zaibatsu made amazing progress, but an overwhelming response from the corporate overlords doomed it to failure. The Chaukis tried to unite native groups with political and labor forces, and for a while it looked like they might stop development and exploitation of some of the last rainforests on Urth. Their connections amazed everyone, for they seemed to have ties to space pilots, indigenous religious figures, military leaders, anarchists and various politicians. The tales of their war have disappeared into the mists of time, but their rebellion failed and their Sathraist allies flew them to Vera Cruz.

TDA unwittingly brought more with them, and strengthened them substantially when they brought more workers from that area to Vera Cruz. The zaibatsu did not realize the Chaukis connection to the old revolutionaries until it was too late, and the Chaukis claimed all its lands. A number of Chaukis had risen to positions of power within TDA, and they used their positions to help this new revolt. Their rise to power on Vera Cruz proved much easier than their fight on Aragon. While some TDA executives and troops resisted, for the most part the takeover proved bloodless, and here the Chaukis claim to nobility came more as a celebration than as a way to rally the populace.

Vera Cruz sent troops to help in the fight on Aragon, and by the time that world fell into Chauki hands, the Diaspora had begun. While numerous noble houses lay claim to parts of Vera Cruz, the Chaukis and we proved superior. Together we brought the planet under one rule, and we did not stop there. Though the Chaukis lacked much in the way of interstellar capabilities, they managed to maintain constant communication with Aragon and sent explorers to other worlds.

My own family continued its own rise to prominence during this time. Some of my ancestors had served with the TDA security forces before seeing the zaibatsu for the evil it really was. We helped the Chaukis dismantle its noxious structure, and we set out to serve the house as its loyal soldiers and advisors. We slowly phased out the unreliable citizens who had infested the army during the uprising against TDA, replacing them with troops trained in honor and loyalty. While many Chaukis had wanted a "citizen militia," Emanuel Primitivo Hazat convinced them of the need for a force such as ours.

For hundreds of years we worked with the Chaukis to create a better, safer life for the people of Vera Cruz and Aragon. We set out to explore Vera Cruz, sending teams deep into its native jungles. Though TDA had imported a number of Terran plants and animals, the planet's native lifeforms remained dominant. The Chaukis encouraged further immigration from Urth, but limited the amount of changes newcomers could make. Thus the planet's jungles remained, and

even during the Diaspora some people turned to a primitive lifestyle. They rejected the technology-ridden cities for the mysterious jungles, and even today, lost tribes occasionally reappear from their depths.

While we initially proposed developing and exploiting the resources found in these jungles, the Chaukis opposed such measures. When the noted terraformer Doramos joined his voices to those calling to preserve the wilderness, we changed our tune. Instead we established our own bases in these distant regions. These military centers avoided the corruption of the Chauki cities and remained pure in their purpose. This remained true even into the days of the Second Republic, whose evil grew within the Chauki holdings.

When the Chaukis called for us to disarm in 3977, we refused. The battles that sprang up on Aragon also spread to Vera Cruz, but here the action was more rapid and decisive. House Chauki knew little of our real strength on this world, and our forces deployed rapidly and intelligently. Highly trained commandos landed in Chauki palaces, and units with special expertise in crowd control quickly moved to prevent any efforts to turn the peasants against us. As on Aragon, the major population centers proved difficult to control, but the rural areas quickly became ours. The local Church proved especially helpful, doing its best to counteract the Chauki propaganda machine.

By the time the actual welfare computers crashed, we had successfully liberated most of Vera Cruz. Thus Vera Cruz proved especially resilient to the hardships the Fall inflicted elsewhere. Our troops moved out to provide food and security to the beleaguered peasantry, offering these in exchange for their labor. Even the plagues that afflicted many worlds after the Fall only had the slightest of effects here. Most families were grateful for the generational contracts we offered them, and their descendants have served us faithfully ever since.

Some, however, threw our generosity back in our faces. These ungrateful wretches sided with their Chauki masters against us, opposing us at every turn. Two areas proved especially difficult to bring under control: the cities where the Chaukis had held power, and the jungles that had given my ancestors comfort for so long. This world offers a host of hiding places, and our enemies made use of many of them.

While we could provide security for most of the planet most of the time, our enemies found ways to leave everyone feeling at risk. Attackers could appear from out of the darkness whenever they pleased, loot and pillage our farms, and disappear again before the full might of our army came to bear. Additionally, noble houses that had claimed land on the planet during the Diaspora rose back up, asserting the same claims once again. Problems continued even after the last Chauki died.

As if these pressures were not enough, the Merchant

League's uprising under Quentin Siegel proved truly dangerous. While we successfully contained them on Sutek and Aragon, Vera Cruz proved more difficult. We greatly underestimated the impact they could have on Vera Cruz. We knew of the Scraver strength on Sutek, and managed to prevent the Muster from being much of a threat on Aragon, but all the guilds proved to be a problem on Vera Cruz.

The League chose the world for a demonstration of its power. Charioteer ships blockaded it, preventing anyone but its allies from even approaching Vera Cruz. Scravers and Reeves made deals with our existing enemies, instigating attack after attack. Finally, Muster mercenaries, supported by the Engineers and their infernal machines, flew into the system. Before we could teach them the error of their ways, however, Patriarch Jacob I laid forth the Privilege of Martyrs doctrine and restored peace.

While this averted war with the League, Vera Cruz's problems continued. The Reeves and Scravers had proven especially effective in agitating the populace, and their covert manipulations created dissension within my house as well as among our peasants. This period also saw the rise of the various branches of the Hazat, as cousins began to feud with one another.

Various family branches already existed, have grown out of the time when we served as the Chaukis' military advisors. The Castenda and Justus lines already held a great deal of influence, but when the Charioteers disrupted travel to Vera Cruz, both had problems maintaining their fiefs. The Bursandra, then a minor lineage, took advantage of the confusion to expand its holdings, using a combination of military might, legal maneuverings and (some say) secret assassinations. By the time any of the other branches could bring in reinforcements from off-world, the Bursandra had seized a majority of the planet.

Raids and counterraids became the order of the day, and the guilds that began these feuds became rich off the hiring of their services for war. Thankfully, before too much havoc occurred, the three leading lines made their peace. This left the Castenda as the leading family on Sutek, the Justus ruling Aragon, and the Bursandra running most of Vera Cruz.

This new harmony was not enough to prevent vicious attacks from a long-forgotten source. These began shortly before the rise of Vladimir, during the 46th century. Ships from unidentified worlds had made their way through the jumpgate before, bringing with them disturbing questions and unwholesome beliefs. Never before had they come in such large numbers, however. Vera Cruz had just recovered from our own internal conflict and these Kurgans, as we learned that they called themselves, made rapid progress.

New battlegrounds appeared across the planet, and we found ourselves face to face with weapons we had forgotten

existed. Their space fighters proved especially troublesome, and they gladly made suicide run after suicide run against our larger ships. Planetary bombardments, anathema during earlier struggles, became the norm, and no one knew when death might rain down on their head. Our enemies also trafficked with occult forces both unholy and deadly, and these fearsome powers stuck terror into our people.

At first, my house reacted slowly to this new threat. Our recent bickering had left fresh wounds, and no one had much interest in helping the Bursandra. But then the threat expanded. Ships made their way through the jumpgate and then raided Aragon and Sutek. The Church became aware of the raiders heretical viewpoints and insisted that they be stopped. Vladimir, whose own house found itself battling raiders on numerous worlds, called for an alliance of noble houses to repel them. While we found his interest in a coalition self-serving at best, we could not ignore its value.

Our forces, combined with those of the other houses, finally turned the tide. In 4547, combined victories in land and space sealed the affair. We caught half of the Kurgan fleet in the Sargasso Belt as it awaited reinforcements. Our cruisers screamed into battle, and most of their carriers were destroyed before they could launch their fighters. Having seized control of space, we attacked the Kurgan stronghold near Karsin. Supported by our own bombardments, we managed to decimate much of their army, driving some of it almost to the northern pole.

Our eyes turned to the lands from which the barbarians came, only to have Vladimir deny us the chance for revenge and expansion. He called for diplomacy with our attackers, but his death ended those plans. Following his assassination (probably arranged by the barbarians he defeated in battle), we launched our own attack on the Kurgan Caliphate. We successfully invaded the one system for which we had a key, only to have the jumproute close on us again. It has opened several times since, and our initial notification each time has come from armed raiders falling from the sky. Our own counteroffensives have to go quickly, for many Hazat have found themselves trapped on the other side when it has closed without warning.

The assaults stopped during the 49th century, and within a few generations became the subject of myth and legend. While the Bursandra maintained troops to repel another raid, they turned more of their attentions to developing their fiefs. Despite occasional disruptions from other houses or branches of our own, the planet became one of those the Church praised for its passivity and its avoidance of progress.

Even the Emperor Wars could not end Vera Cruz's serenity. While the Bursandra initially opposed Prince Juan Jacobi Nelson Eduardo de Aragon's rise to power, they quickly saw the wisdom in supporting him — shortly after they saw his armada come through their jumpgate. Indeed, Vera Cruz

proved important to the Hazat war effort in many ways. It supplied numerous legions of enthusiastic troops, fed our armies and provided special areas for our troops to rest and train, safe from enemy attack. We took advantage of its distance from the frontlines to create training camps that became the model for those the Imperial Legions use today. I trained at some of these myself, including one rumored to host our famed Dervishes. Of course, I saw nothing untoward there.

Despite the military strength deployed on Vera Cruz, my house proved unprepared for the reappearance of an ancient enemy. In 4987, while the Emperor Wars distracted us, the Kurgans reappeared. It seemed that they could fly back and forth with impunity, while every expedition we took to their lands cost us gravely. Thankfully, our first expedition to Hira revealed the descendants of Hazat from previous wars, still doing battle against the heretics. Their assistance proved instrumental in holding back the tide of heathens waiting beyond the gate.

Following the peace with you, my Emperor, we could turn the full weight of our military might against the Kurgans, and we drove them from Vera Cruz. While the planet has since seen some more unrest, especially when we disbanded our Dervish legions, it has begun to revert to its peaceful state from before the Kurgan attacks.

Solar System

Puebla: This planet is smaller than many moons, but that has not stopped innumerable groups from fighting for its mineral wealth. This has long been a contentious planet, and even today the Charioteers, Scravers, Li Halan and the Church make claims to our property.

Vera Cruz: Some optimists say that the fading suns phenomenon has made Vera Cruz a better place to live, and its temperature has definitely become more moderate over the last several centuries. While it has its share of industry, much of the planet has remained undeveloped, and jungles cover thousands of acres of land.

Albemarle: During the Diaspora, a number of zaibatsu conducted secret experiments here, and the planet has never recovered. Radioactive hot spots dot the landscape thousands of years later, and the water that sat at its poles is now corrupt and noxious. The Second Republic made some effort to clean it up, but it did little other than add more debris to the world.

Pharis (Hanbar, Squire Bourbon): This small gas giant features two large moons and several smaller ones. Hanbar used to be a recreation stop for space crews, and during the late Diaspora it became known as a place where anything was permitted. Now it lies abandoned, most of its buildings scavenged after the Fall. Squire Bourbon has been home to the Bourbon minor house since the Chaukis gave

them this moon. They added a distillery to their holdings about a century ago, but have a problem finding both the parts and raw materials to keep it operating. These nobles keep to themselves as much as possible, and ties to space pirates have never been proven.

Sargasso Belt: The Sargasso Belt actually encompasses several different asteroid belts in the farther parts of Vera Cruz space. At various times, innumerable stops existed here for Kurgans, pirates, smugglers and adventurers. Every time we think we have cleaned them all out, more pop up.

Katara: This small planet's orbit keeps it near the jumpgate, so it serves as a refueling point and arms depot for our space fleet. The Kurgans have attacked it a number of times, but have never been able to wipe it out completely.

People and Places

The Vera Cruz spaceport has changed since I first visited this world as a youth. Back then it primarily served traders and nobles, with cruise ships coming and going despite the Emperor Wars, and merchants making the highly profitable run from Sutek to Vera Cruz to Aragon to Byzantium Secundus and back to Sutek. While many troops made their way through its loading areas, I remember these soldiers as clean and polished, fresh from their training camps or from well-deserved rests.

Now soldiers seem to make up the majority of spaceport visitors, and these are not the crisp and clean warriors of my youth. Though the fighting on Hira has gone well, we still suffer casualties. Vera Cruz offers the wounded their best source of solace… and the dead their final resting-place. The troops looking to leave are harried and nervous, scared by stories they have heard about the war on Hira… or the ones they have already experienced. Veterans from the Emperor Wars have known nothing but war for years, and many want nothing more than to leave the service. Their replacements seem too young for the job.

When the Kurgans began raiding this system more than a decade ago, they disrupted the trade routes, and the luxury liners only visit when the military escorts them. We fortified the spaceport as best we could, and now it resembles nothing as much as the armed camps that sprung up around Byzantium Secundus during the Emperor Wars. When I arrived on the planet, troops did not greet me as they did on Aragon, but more of them milled about.

I did meet with Baron Ukuta Holdea Mto de Amani, whose Paragon Squadron of destroyers and frigates provides the system's quickest response to any threat. He said that while no large incursions of Kurgan warships have occurred in the past several years, the number of individual ships passing through the gate has increased — and these have a better chance of slipping through our jumpgate blockade. He fears that more than a few of these ships have made it all

21

the way to Vera Cruz. He also believes that at least a few of these ships have not been Kurgan, and may have come from the Known Worlds, independent space, or even the Vuldrok Star-Nation. In addition, he promised to help track down whatever ship may have brought St. Belchair's scepter.

My quest for Rucka Jamon de Luista then took me to the capital at Los Aztecha. I sought out Baron Sabrea Navaja Carcel de Bursandra, with whom I trained during the Emperor Wars. By the time the Wars had ended, he had a well-deserved reputation as a tactician and leader of men, and I hoped that he could tell me something about Rucka. Despite our previous friendship, Baron Sabrea proved very reluctant to talk about him. While I failed to get any details from the baron, he did direct me away from the capital and south, to the small village of Los Triaja.

Here I found a good bit of squalor and poverty, but at first, I saw no sign of Rucka. Then I began to see the subtle differences between this hamlet and a normal one. Many of Los Triaja's residents had obviously served in the military, but they did not have the proud bearing of most of our ex-soldiers. Instead, they had the beaten, haggard appearance of prisoners of war. Many of them had obvious scars, signs of badly treated wounds. Additionally, none of them really seemed comfortable in their village, as if it were not really theirs. At first I thought that Los Triaja provided a haven for soldiers who had suffered the worst of the Emperor Wars,

but its lack of healers made me doubt that. Then I noticed that even the town's priest was a battered veteran.

This priest, Novitiate Martene Iglesia, at first proved extremely reluctant to talk to me, but with the aid of a bottle of Aragonian red, and the constant reassurances of Sister Halva, he finally poured out his tale. Martene, like most of the residents of Los Triaja, did not originate here. As a child, he had evidenced psychic abilities, and my family selected him early to serve as one of our elite Dervishes. He trained with some of our greatest military instructors, who brought his talents to a peak. His mastery of psychic paths, as well as his extensive training, made him perfect for a wide variety of duties. As a result, he fought on many planets, handling any role his commanders might give him.

During his travels, he became aware of a group within the Dervishes calling themselves the Order of the Serpent and Peacock. While he swears that he never joined its ranks, many of his friends and comrades did. He believes that by the time the war ended, at least one in four of our Dervishes had enrolled in the Order. At the end of the Emperor Wars, the Church pressured my house to disband the Dervishes and forbid their further association. I do not know if this was because of the Order or just due to its fear of psychic soldiers, but after some resistance, my house complied.

We ordered the Dervish legions disbanded, quietly mustered out its members, and ordered them to never again as-

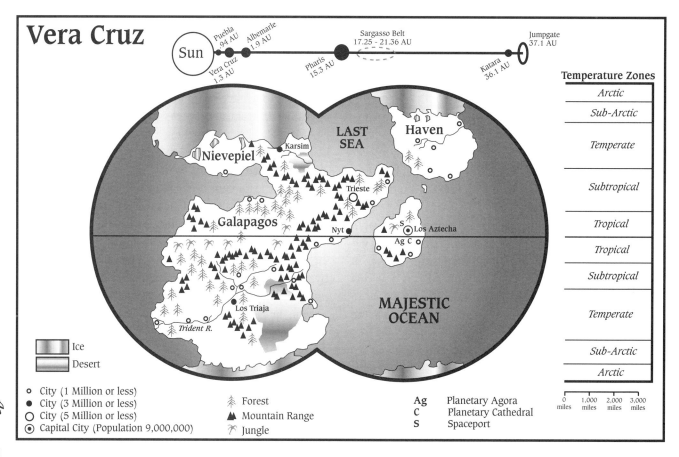

Vera Cruz

Sun	
Puebla 94 AU	
Vera Cruz 1.3 AU	
Albemarle 1.9 AU	
Pharis 15.3 AU	
Sargasso Belt 17.25 - 21.36 AU	
Katara 36.1 AU	
Jumpgate 37.1 AU	

LAST SEA

Haven

Karsim

Nievepiel

Trieste

Galapagos

Nyt

Los Aztecha

Ag C

S

Los Triaja

Trident R.

MAJESTIC OCEAN

Temperature Zones

Arctic
Sub-Arctic
Temperate
Subtropical
Tropical
Tropical
Subtropical
Temperate
Sub-Arctic
Arctic

Ice
Desert

	0	1,000	2,000	3,000
		miles	miles	miles

o   City (1 Million or less)
●   City (3 Million or less)
○   City (5 Million or less)
◉   Capital City (Population 9,000,000)

🌲   Forest
▲   Mountain Range
🌴   Jungle

Ag   Planetary Agora
C   Planetary Cathedral
S   Spaceport

sociate or use their psychic abilities — upon pain of death. We offered them substantial retirement bonuses, but fear immediately swept their ranks. Martene believes that the Order promoted this fear, spreading rumors that we intended to register all of them with the Inquisition. Martene's story became a jumble at this point, blaming the rebellion that followed on all manner of causes:

- A faction of Hazat angry with the treaty that ended the Emperor Wars and hoping for another chance to fight;
- Hawkwood spies spreading dissension within our ranks;
- Church officials hoping for a reason to make all the Dervishes penitent psychics;
- Kurgan infiltrators looking to destroy one of our key military assets; and
- The Order of the Serpent and Peacock, which had some greater goal that required our Dervishes stay together.

Whatever the cause, the results are not in doubt. Many of the Dervishes refused to disband, and they seized several arsenals in order to equip themselves for battle. My house saw this as an extreme threat. The Dervishes could not only cause a great deal of damage to Vera Cruz (where they were based), but they could disrupt our war efforts against the Kurgan Caliphate and attract far too much attention from the Inquisition. We moved quickly to stop the threat.

The same instructors and commanders who had formed the Dervishes now lead the efforts to destroy them. Such noted warriors as Don Marchenko Catilla Arronto Justus, Don Marcika Holuzio Rolas, and Doña Silvia Shondra Bursandra led the campaign against the renegade Dervishes, soldiers with whom they had once served. Most people on Vera Cruz never knew the battles ever took place, even though fighting sometimes broke out in the heart of its few urban centers, such as Trieste and Nyt.

Martene's feelings of betrayal and loss became obvious as he told us about desperate, bloody battles, with no quarter asked or given. He tried to hide his emotions, but an utter sense of despair slowly came over him. The Serpent and the Peacock had offered him something great, some kind of self-knowledge that he desperately sought. What he told me of its teachings reminded me somewhat of tales of the Brother Battle I have heard. These were tales of a close connection to the Pancreator brought about through intense exercises — physical, mental and spiritual. It also involved tasks assigned by the more "enlightened" members of the order to guide others toward spiritual growth.

Martene believes Rucka Jamon de Luista helped form and lead the Order of the Serpent and Peacock. When my house finally defeated the rebels, many of them died, while the rest were scattered, first to prison camps and then to villages like Los Triaja, where we could keep a very close eye on them. Not all of the village's inhabitants were former

Dervishes. The remainder were their allies and troops. My house kept them in check with constant medicines and drugs, both to dampen their powers and to ensure that they would not rise up again, unless humanity had a pressing need for their special powers. Not many of the Dervishes escaped their punishment, but Rucka (and several of the other leaders) did. Martene had a good idea of where Rucka might be — the deepest jungles of Vera Cruz.

I spent the next several months exploring these shadowy rainforests. While I spent some time in the beautiful cities of Los Aztecha, Vera Cruz's island capital, I spent far more in its humid interior. As you know from previous letters, I discovered a number of lost tribes in areas civilized people have not traveled for centuries. Some of these tribes still worshipped the Pancreator, while others had their own, far more bizarre religions.

I also had several encounters with bandits in the mountain regions. I pitied these poor men and women, for most of them had served my house during the Emperor Wars, but now found themselves unable to support themselves upon their return. Their farms either had been given to other serfs or had become barren, forcing them to lives of theft and robbery. It gave me no pleasure to cut them down.

However, one such bandit group did turn out to have an ex-Dervish leader. He directed me to the ancient Naturae convent in the arctic. Sister Halva's help proved again invaluable, for I was the first man allowed to stay there in more than 200 years. However, I was hardly its first male visitor during that time.

The sisters insisted that I stay, and I joined them in their meditations and prayer. I have never enjoyed such a period of peace and contentment, and I could feel the Pancreator's love around me at all times. My burning desire for St. Belchair's scepter waned for a few days, and for the first time during these travels I felt myself relax. Then Rucka visited me.

He appeared at 3 a.m., shortly before morning meditations. He woke me as I slept on the mat provided by the sisters, and I knew at once who I faced. He drew a knife, and I leapt immediately to the attack. I have long considered myself capable in the martial arts, and it gave me great pride when you, my Emperor, asked me to instruct other Questing Knights in their practice. Rucka had many of the same teachers as I, and while I managed to land my initial blows, our fight quickly became a series of blocked attacks and interrupted counterattacks. At first I tried to call for aid, but the slightest hesitation on my part brought his knife across my neck, and I turned my concentration completely to the battle at hand.

I do not know how long we fought, with me twisting and turning to avoid his knife, and him barely avoiding the blows that could have broken his bones or numbed his limbs.

All I knew was that I was covered in cuts and blood, and bruises had begun to form all across his body. Then Prioress Sofia Joya appeared in the doorway. Her tirade against Rucka seemed to hit him with more force than any of my blows, and both of us froze in the face of her righteous wrath.

She commanded Rucka tell me the reason for his attack, and I saw a horrible strain overcome him as he fought the holy compulsion under which she placed him. Finally, he threw himself in a heap at her feet and admitted to having been hired to kill me. His patron? Don Siccaro Petard Castenda, who once sought me as his page. Don Siccaro now had the relic, and had taken it to Hira. I could not bring Rucka to justice, for the prioress said the redemption of his soul was a matter for the Church, not the courts. I believe that she may have been his instructor before, for he addressed her as such several times. He is a mighty warrior, and I hope that she will bring him back to the Holy Flame. As for me, I now had to plunge into the heart of the heretics, and continue my quest on Hira.

Hira

I may well be acting too soon in calling Hira a Hazat world, but our strength has finally made itself felt. Our dedicated and well-trained legions have driven the Kurgan troops from most of its surface, and we have begun the process of adding its people to our fold. Of course, with Hira nothing is ever sure, for we have made progress before only to see the jumpgate close.

Also, while we believe that we have driven much of the Kurgan military from the planet, my recent experience on this war-torn world leaves me doubting that it is really under our control — or whether it ever can be. Its residents may pay their taxes to our troops, but I do not think they give their loyalty to anybody.

History

Hira has always been a world of mystery, with key parts of its history a blank to our scholars. That an alliance of extreme technophiles first settled the planet during the early Diaspora is undeniable, though it attempted to keep its early operations a secret. It established numerous research facilities and sought to tear Hira's many secrets from her grasp. It conducted a myriad of experiments on its fauna and flora, sought to reach the depths of its seas, and even attempted to probe to the heart of the world itself.

Since explorers did not discover Hira until the final days of the First Republic, no single zaibatsu ever dominated the planet. A number of them sent out corporate teams, but their problems back on Holy Terra prevented any serious efforts. While a number of zaibatsu sponsored the original settlers, they found themselves unable to control them. The technophiles used their connections with Terran universities and scholars to oppose zaibatsu attempts to expand their grasp. Just to ensure zaibatsu difficulty in coming to Hira, the technophiles opened the planet to colonization by independent Terran groups.

Colonists flocked to Hira, drawn by its open spaces and freedom from zaibatsu control. They settled the best land, making it more difficult for the zaibatsu to exert its influence. However, the technophiles were not content with just creating an independent world. With the First Republic no longer a threat, they sought to make the world a scientific utopia, but instead paid the price for such hubris.

The comet Mirzabah slammed into the jumpgate well before the technophiles could create a self-sufficient society, and Hira's circumstances quickly degenerated. Cut off from the still-necessary trade ships, ships that brought everything from building supplies to think machines to the most basic of consumer goods, society quickly collapsed. While records from most of this period either disappeared or never existed, we know that the new colonists fought with the technophiles. While scholars remain unsure of the specific causes of their feud, an old Hiran told me that the colonists believe the technophiles actually caused the comet to shut down the jumpgate. Additionally, the colonists also thought the technophiles were hiding things from them, though I have not learned whether this refers to a stash of consumer goods or something more ominous.

The technophiles may well have believed their high-tech weapons and defenses would protect them, but the colonists had many of the same items. They quickly overwhelmed the technophiles, driving the survivors into Hira's jungles, where they undoubtedly perished. The colonists then turned on one another, and within a generation had reduced to barbarism.

Records from this time are scarce, but we do know that several small "empires" rose and fell during this time. Since Hira's population never grew especially large, I have a hard time calling any of these "empires". One that did grow especially large was the M'Ballah culture, a collection of various ethnic groups from Urth united behind the ideal of someday rejoining humanity. It rose and fell on the Juruta continent, but made a great effort to preserve its records when decline

became inevitable. While the Second Republic recovered many of the M'Ballah's records, Brother Battle monks recently discovered several treasure troves of M'Ballah books. We hope to find more soon.

When the jumproute reopened to Hira during the early days of the Second Republic, it failed to excite much interest. While many planets had created strong societies and industrial bases during the Diaspora, Hira had slid into its own brand of primitivism. The corporations made half-hearted efforts to sell their goods to its inhabitants, but the Hirans had little worth trading. The planet might have been written off as an unprofitable backwater except for the exciting scientific finds that kept cropping up.

Its native attributes again attracted scientists of all hues, but the most exciting find happened off-planet, near the planet Mirzabah, believed to be the heart of the giant comet that had slammed into the jumpgate but was now trapped in orbit around the sun. Here they found a missing piece of the jumpgate itself. The planet became a magnet for xenotechnologists from across human space, and rumor has it that even the Vau took an interest in this system.

Of course, the Chaukis also seized the opportunity to expand their power. Due to Hira's proximity to Vera Cruz, the Chaukis took the lead in developing its industry and natural resources. Under the guise of attempting to reincorporate Hira into the human community, the House Chauki developed giant farms and mining operations, established hospitals and transportation networks, and spent a great deal of money in expanding the spaceport the Second Republic built.

Again the Chaukis tried to limit my own ancestors' involvement in their activities, hoarding the wealth gained here for themselves. They claimed that the world had no need of a strong military presence, and that my ancestors should limit themselves to helping the populace police itself. Of course, this left the world open to more nefarious influences. Kurgan interest in Hira seems to stem from this period.

As early as the 38th century, the travel lanes between Kurgan territory and Hira bustled with activity. Ancient Charioteer documents show lost worlds named Irem and Tsuma from which a great deal of merchant and personal travel to Hira originated. Apparently, these now make up the heart of the Kurgan Caliphate. Its corruptive influence quickly became apparent, as Kurgan styles of dress and entertainment became popular with the native population.

By the time our problems with the Chaukis turned into armed conflict, the Chaukis had become the planet's dominant landowners. However, their actual presence was rather limited. They had turned much of the planet over to native oversight under some misguided attempt to make the planet more self-reliant. While we also lacked much military strength on Hira, our local police had kept tabs on all the

Hira Traits

Cathedral: Avestite
Agora: Muster
Garrison: 7
Capital: Fort Omala
Jumps: 3
Adjacent Worlds: Vera Cruz (dayside), Khayyam (nightside)
Solar System: Falai (.68 AU), Hira (.96 AU; Ulalumn), Korbuchuk (14 AU), Eslemiel (31 AU), Mirzabah (37 AU), Jumpgate (38 AU)
Tech: 2
Human Population: 400,000,000
Alien Population: Unknown
Resources: Contraband, relics
Exports: Tubaq, qoqa, Ayuwazat vine, vials of the blood of Baronet Teikorc, fingerbones of St. Ruthus, splinters from the coffin of Don Gonzago, weapons from various lost warriors and monks.
Landscape: Five continents dominate Hira: Teikorc and Juruta in the southern hemisphere, Givral and Daanyu in the north, and Halalaj straddling the equator. Hira's main geographical feature — immediately noticeable from orbit — is its equatorial rainforest, spanning three continents with a canopy five layers deep at its center.

Chaukis. We rounded them up as quickly as possible, but found that the local populace did not appreciate our efforts.

Much of this unhappiness seemed to emanate from the Kurgan worlds, and we quickly moved to curtail their unhealthy influence. With the aid of Church ships and captains, we interdicted the jumpgate, searching ships for Chauki sympathizers and turning back Kurgan vessels. Only recently have we discovered what happened to these valiant soldiers.

Kurgan warriors, lead by an ancient entertainer whose image still appears in Known World magic lantern shows, blasted past our blockade and landed on Mirzabah. There they seized the jumpgate fragment in order to work the most foul of magic upon it. They managed to close the jumpgate, preventing our reinforcements from getting through. Then this entertainer made use of her strongest manipulative abilities to rally the system against us. Our soldiers fought valiantly but could not hope to win against all their opponents. Battles raged on every planet of the system, but finally the last of our troops surrendered, many never to be heard from again.

While many scholars are now pouring over the records from this time and during the period of Kurgan control, we still know little of what went on here. That society again degenerated is a certainty. With the jumpgate again deacti-

vated, the planet declined even more than it did during the Diaspora. Much of it fell into rudimentary tool use, its people unable to even comprehend the many devices left by the Second Republic.

Those areas that avoided this fate seem to have been those most influenced by the Kurgans, which leads many to believe that the Kurgans orchestrated the planet's decline. The area that remained the most technically efficient, the lands around Dal Jimbalif, became the center of Kurgan culture on Hira.

In 4327, omens revealed that the jumpgate had again opened, and the Justus branch of my family mounted an expedition to re-enlighten this darkened world. Don Gonzago Justus led this effort, but within a year the jumpgate closed again. Despite the deactivation, Don Gonzago managed to establish a Hazat fief that has survived to this very day. This Andalus fief attracted many natives to its protective walls, including those who had descended from our earlier military presence.

Actual Kurgan assaults against our growing fief did not occur for more than a century, but from that point on they proved relentless. While the earliest Kurgan efforts were primarily directed against Vera Cruz, Andalus also saw some fighting. We made as many forays to Hira as we could, but had to devote most of our military might to defending Vera Cruz. After Vladimir came to power, and the threat to Vera Cruz receded, we prepared to relieve Andalus. The time seemed ripe, for Kurgan losses had created a great deal of unrest on Hira. Vladimir, however, blocked this glorious mission. He insisted on attempting a diplomatic solution — one we knew the Kurgans would taint and twist.

After Vladimir's death, we again prepared to relieve Hira, but our military became increasingly involved in the many feuds that his death spawned. By the time we could concentrate our attention on Hira, the jumproute to Vera Cruz closed. With its line to our strength broken, Andalus suffered horribly from Kurgan attacks. Numerous Hazat heroes grew out of this period, however, and their monumental efforts proved the difference between life and death for Andalus.

Such warriors as Don Pared Corbata de Tracha, Doña Devesta Pera Bursandra, and Baronet Cama Novia Cepilla Justus gave all they could for the glory of our house. Don Pared stopped several massive Kurgan assaults through the mountain passes of Teikorc (the continent Kurgans still call Imbuk). Doña Devesta created the navy and air force that kept us safe from two directions. Baronet Cama mounted a heroic campaign that broke a Kurgan siege of Shelit and brought House Shelit over to our side.

This native house proved invaluable in stopping later Kurgan aggressions, and our alliance with it has benefited both of us. While some Avestites whisper that the Shelit's affinity to technology is not natural, and that the house may

well have descended from Hira's original technophile settlers, I do not believe it. However, Sir Nin Shelit, a doer within the house and one of your own Questing Knights, has told me that the house does have legends of Vau visits dating back to the Second Republic.

Whatever the truth, our alliance with the Shelit helped make Andalus more resistant to Kurgan invasion. The Shelit and their serfs supplied us with weapons almost as good as those of the Known Worlds, and repaired those we brought from Vera Cruz. Still, the war against the Kurgans remained a holding action until the jumpgate reopened during the Emperor Wars.

The pressure against Andalus lightened almost immediately as the Kurgans concentrated their military against Vera Cruz. Thus, when one of our ships went through the jumpgate and landed on Hira, we found a strong army just itching for action. With our spaceships and the Andalus troops, we managed to launch an offensive that expanded Hazat holdings for the first time since Don Gonzago landed on the planet. The Kurgans had to curtail their own attacks on Vera Cruz to deal with this new threat, but we never let up on the pressure.

The key point came with our glorious defense during the Siege of Omala. We managed to seize the ancient spaceport and held it against repeated Kurgan counterattacks. Many Hazat and Shelit knights died during this effort, including the valiant Baronet Teikorc, but our forces held. Soon we began ferrying reinforcements and equipment through the port, and our position was secure.

Following the end of the Emperor Wars, we could finally devote ourselves to freeing Hira and keeping Vera Cruz safe from Kurgan attacks. Legion after legion of trained veterans embarked for Hira. While far too many of these died along the way, the victims of Kurgan space fighters, enough made it to the planet to allow us to take the offensive. Our initial push took us onto the Juruta continent, but our growing dominance in space allowed us to mount attacks wherever we pleased. Within a year, our assault landers had dropped troops on every continent on Hira, including the Kurgan center of power on Daanyu.

While the Kurgans are our main enemies, we never know whether other native groups will prove helpful, neutral or hostile. Those with the closest ties to the Kurgans still oppose us, fighting us whenever they get the chance. Most of the people seem indifferent, offering us the same tribute they gave the Kurgans. Some have welcomed us, especially after having visits from Church missionaries… and Inquisitors.

By 4999, most of the Juruta continent had come under our sway. Battles between the jumpgate and Hira decreased as less and less Kurgan ships braved the journey. Associates on Hira have told me that the Caliph's popularity within the Caliphate has waned, and my house's own agents have helped spread dissension on other worlds beyond the jumpgate. I have no idea just how extensive these rebellions beyond Hira might be, but they have no doubt lessened the heretics' ability to do battle. Still, they fought ferociously when we began the Girata offensive of 5000, which established our control of most of Hira. The Kurgans remain in power on Daanyu, however, and the battle there will no doubt prove deadly.

The planet will not truly belong to us until the Kurgan capital of Dal Jimbalif falls, and even then, the heathens may keep fighting. They have shown an amazing level of perseverance in the face of adversity. Most of the war has involved unconventional fighting of the worst type, with hit-and-run actions the order of the day. Only recently did the Kurgans begin meeting our legions in the field, and our progress stems from that.

Solar System

Falai: We made this cloudy, wind-ravaged world a secret supply point during the war, knowing that the Kurgans would keep searching the more distant planets for our marshalling area. We have since moved most of our equipment to Hira, but some lords want to establish small industrial fiefs here.

Hira (Ulaumn): I like this bright, clear world. It has a fresher smell than do most worlds I have visited, and its native life forms are both beautiful and useful. Even its moon shines more brilliantly in the sky than any I remember, despite the many soldiers who have died on its surface.

Korbuchuk: Battles have raged around this gas giant on a number of occasions, though the nomads who inhabit one of its larger moons have done their best to remain neutral. Our navy still finds pockets of Kurgan resistance on some of the dozens of moons that orbit Korbuchuk.

Eslemiel: Few fights have taken place around this smaller gas giant, for its moons offer little to anyone. Our explorers have sought out rumors of Second Republic installations here, but so far have had no luck.

Mirzabah: The jumpgate fragment discovered here during the Second Republic is long gone, as is most interest in the world. Recently, however, our ships intercepted a Kurgan galliot orbiting this tiny planet. There is some evidence that it unloaded a number of troops on the planet, but we have not been able to find them.

People and Places

I disembarked on Hira with a great deal of trepidation. Not only was it a planet still at war, but this was the land where my parents met their inglorious end, defending Fort Omala. When people speak of Fort Omala, they generally refer to the inner walls where Baronet Teikorc met his end.

It refers to much more than just that stronghold. It really encompasses the spaceport and several large barracks and administration areas, and other urban areas are growing up around it.

The spaceport itself boasts some massive armament, including massive planet-to-space lasers seized from the Kurgans. Their weapons have a distinctly foreign look to them, and Fort Omala itself has an appearance unique among Hazat cities. While most of the Kurgan structures suffered extreme damage during (and after) the siege, enough remain to give the city an alien feel. Odd clay buildings, minarets, giant domed buildings and more prove its uniqueness, though I have seen similar buildings on Istakhr.

The city, and most of the world, bustles with military activity. Troops travel hither and thither, and every other cart and vehicle seems packed with their equipment. The Church makes its presence felt everywhere, and priests of all stripes have poured into the city. Some treat our troops, missionaries who seek to convert the natives; others look for relics among Kurgan ruins, and more than a few join us in the war. Makeshift churches have sprung up everywhere, as have the less wholesome industries that seem to follow an army. I find the existence of so many brothels and bars especially amazing considering the vast array of Avestites and similar zealots, though some joke that these holy people traffic in such establishments even more than do the soldiers.

After prayer and confession at Purita Chapel, near the site of the great siege, I sought out my parents' grave. Tombstones and monuments circle Fort Omala, but my parents' resting-place required a great deal of searching to locate. Only a simple stone engraved with a jumpgate cross marks it. This by itself marks it as distinctive, for we have presented our dead with elaborate markers whenever possible. Still, I am happy with this small tribute, for witnesses said they saw my parents trying to flee Fort Omala before the final offensive. They died in a crossfire between our troops and the Kurgans, and we did not recover their bodies for several days. My family had believed the Kurgans took the scepter of St. Belchair until I heard rumors of it still being on Sutek. My prayers at their grave provided no guidance, but I felt much better for having finally done so.

My next visit was to the Crested Dome, a former Kurgan temple my house has turned into one of our headquarters. It proved a madhouse of activity, with troops, priests, messengers and Muster executives dashing back and forth. My arrival on Hira coincided with our Givral offensive, so Fort Omala hosted even more troops than usual. I sought out Duke Bellosyte Armane Korlat Spetara Rolas, one of the few military leaders on this world willing to correspond with me after my family's infamous deed.

From his small office, located in what his aide told me

was once a Caliphate penance cell, he directed the efforts of several ground legions in the assault. He knew of Don Siccaro Petard Castenda, but said that the Don now commanded one of our frontline positions in the war. While I initially hoped to confront Don Siccaro immediately, the duke sought to dissuade me of this course. The offensive had just begun, and the Don's legion held a critical point along our flank by the Sea of Tsulu. The duke indicated that he would not appreciate any action that might undermine its stability.

I offered him my aid, a proposal he had to consider for some time. Despite his obvious need for more swords, my family's sullied reputation worried him. Finally, he asked if I would assist him on a quieter matter. Rumors had reached him of Hazat conspiring with our enemies, and he asked my entourage to help investigate such matters. Of course, my cohorts and I agreed.

I took a great risk by quietly spreading the word that I wanted to meet with the Kurgans. Here my family's own infamy helped, as did local Imperial Eye agents. My quest took me across much of Hira, from the Shelit's bizarre metallic castles to the bombed ruins of Hiran villages to ancient Diasporan facilities, long ago swallowed by the jungle. I encountered refugees and deserters from both sides of the war, all desperate for whatever they could steal. Ancient experiments (and some more recent) have twisted some of the planet's original creatures, and these mutated beasts still inhabit some of the facilities to which we journeyed. Golems, whether escaped from the Shelit or from Diasporan installations, also proved a hazard.

Finally, in the ruins of an ancient menagerie on the Hwilayt Archipelago, a Kurgan who called himself Purga Buran offered me a chance for revenge against the Hazat who killed my parents. He claimed to know of a meeting between certain rogue Hazat and members of the Caliphate going on in an ancient observatory. He and I immediately set out by boat for a small island near Hira's arctic region. We sailed past military craft of both forces, and even passed within a mile of a fierce naval engagement, but no one ever saw us.

The observatory island also proved busy, with several large ships docked in front, and large numbers of people visible on the land. Purga maneuvered the craft into an isolated cove and into a cave that I could not see until we were mere feet from it. The cave turned into a series of tunnels that led us right to the base of the observatory. While Second Republic craftsmanship does little to impress me, this observatory did. A massive structure, its very solidity seemed both reassuring and imposing. Something about it seemed to belie the irreligious feeling I get from most Second Republic buildings, and I would have knelt in prayer had not Purga hurried me through a secret door.

The passage beyond the door took us through room after room filled with unidentifiable machinery. The efforts of my trip, combined with my stunning surroundings, began to make me feel light-headed, and I was about to insist on stopping when Purga announced that we had reached our destination. He identified himself to a retinal scanner, made some hand gestures while muttering arcane sounds, and a door I had not seen slid open.

He motioned for me to enter, and I cautiously advanced. Upon passing the doorway, it felt as if I was trying to walk through Artemisian grass jelly. It took an effort just to move my head in time to see the bizarre array of figures charging at me. Two-headed goat beings, human-like insects and floating limbs all made their way for me. Farther ahead, I could see a number of people, both Kurgan and Hazat, surrounding a Kurgan who seemed to move as slow as I did.

I battled this freakish array of foes as best I could, but every blow I struck seemed to make me weaker, nauseous, and disoriented. Despite my disorientation, I could hear Purga as he began to chant in Latin. I could not make out all his words, but I did hear him ask someone to accept his two sacrifices, and to help him desecrate the land where we stood. I tried to aim my blaster at him, but his grotesque minions seemed to intercept each one, blowing apart as they saved him.

Finally they knocked my blaster from my hand, and I saw them overwhelm the Kurgan at the same time. The Kurgan's last effort had been to throw a grenade, but I saw that the pin was still in it. I dove for the grenade before recognizing its type — a sonic screamer. I felt my last hope disappear, for such a nonlethal weapon would only delay my death, not prevent it. Still, I had no other weapons left, so I pulled its pin, threw it toward Purga, and covered my ears.

Despite my attempt at protection, my head felt as though someone had driven mammoth barbed spikes into it. I fell, writhing in agony, unable to prevent the doom ready to befall me — a doom that did not come. Instead, the pain began to melt away, and I saw the Kurgan tearing through our enemies as if they did not exist. Indeed, the bizarre opponents I had faced no longer existed, their place taken by more humans. Their agony from the grenade obviously exceeded my own, for they put up little resistance. The Kurgan seemed completely unaffected, and reached Purga without difficulty. Before anything else could happen, however, Purga's head disintegrated in a red haze that surprised the Kurgan as much as it surprised me. The Kurgan, who now revealed herself as Fahim Sinai, and I rounded up his accomplices with little difficulty.

Together we led them outside, where nearby guards gasped in amazement as we appeared from where they thought no entrance existed. I was also taken into custody, though Fahim insisted that I be treated as a guest. Her words

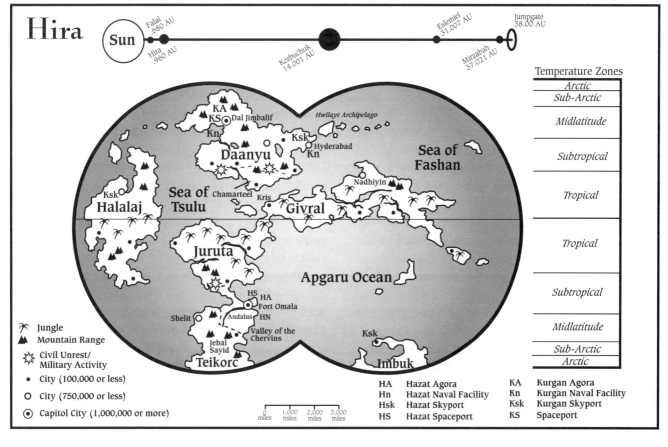

carried weight, and I later learned that she serves the Caliph as one of his Blessed, an elite warrior. Purga had caught her while she investigated charges of rogue Kurgans associating with Hazat. By the end of the day, more Kurgan officials landed on the island. I met such high-ranking officers of the Caliphate as Atabeg Palu Hassan Fatuma, security chief for the archipelago, and Imam Mabhu Yusuf Abdamahah, head of the observatory and a surprisingly powerful man for such a post.

I spent almost a month among the Kurgans, both as a prisoner and as a guest. They hurried me off the island, however, taking me to Hyderabad on the Daanyu continent. The Kurgans did their best to keep me from seeing the military preparations taking place there, but I managed to make some observations of a nearby spaceport. Kurgan spaceships remind me of nothing so much as giant metallic insects, and they seemed to swarm over Hyderabad. They seemed to remove as many people as they landed, and for every soldier I saw them disgorge, they removed at least one civilian. At first, I thought the Kurgans were evacuating Hira prior to my house's conquest. As I studied the evacuees, I noticed that they appeared to herald from a variety of worlds, and that they seemed happy to be traveling, not the sullen refugees I have seen elsewhere. In fact, they had the appearance of pilgrims I have seen returning from a visit to Holy Terra — quietly ecstatic, and with almost a holy glow about them.

I met regularly with Fahim Sinai, who seemed especially interested in the rumors I had followed of traitorous meetings between our peoples. Our investigations had convinced both of us that these rendezvous involved far more than just attempts to subvert our respective armies. Sinai indicated that the observatory held great religious significance for her people, and that the ritual we disrupted aimed to open the site to unholy forces. She and I agreed to share information about these meetings, and she helped engineer the "escape" that brought me back to Hazat territory.

The escape, which involved me stealing a small hovercraft and sailing to Givraal, ended when a fierce storm sent my vehicle spiraling into a rocky cliff. After swimming to shore, I found myself on the outskirts of a fierce fight between my house and the Caliphate, and had to fight through retreating Kurgan troops to reach the battlefield. I surrendered to our own troops, a maneuver that almost proved fatal, and I realized just how often soldiers in battle refuse to take prisoners. It proved even more dangerous when I learned that Don Siccaro commanded my captors.

Mindful of Duke Bellosyte's request that I not hinder the war effort in any way, I made no reference to his theft of the scepter. He seemed happy to see me, and immediately offered me a leadership position among his forces. I accepted, especially after he made it clear just how intense the fighting had become. Our forces faced stiffened resistance all along the front, and the troops I had seen landing near Hyderabad had now taken the field.

Don Siccaro planned an assault for the very next day, and I took command of a platoon in his shock legion. Unfortunately, my troops and I quickly discovered that our artillery had been programmed with incorrect attack plans, and soon Hazat shells rained down on our heads. I had anticipated such a problem, however, and took my troops along an alternate route — one that also avoided an unmarked mine field in our path. My alternate route, discovered when I had earlier slipped through Kurgan lines, brought us to the flank of the point of our attack. Our initial probes proved that the Kurgans had reinforced this point to an extreme degree, and my platoon had little chance of breaking through it. Instead, we slipped behind it, for our main objective was to take a hill behind this hardpoint.

We seized the hill without difficulty and began to entrench. The Kurgans soon realized what we had done, and within an hour had begun to attack us from all sides. We suffered heavy losses while repelling their assaults, and might have failed had not the bulk of the Hazat assault finally reached our location. The fact that we had disrupted the hardpoint by taking the hill behind it was the only reason our forces could penetrate this far. However, as soon as the Brother Battle troops leading the assault reached our hill, they placed me under arrest for consorting with the enemy, and imprisoned the remainder of my platoon as well. Only then did I discover that the platoon I had commanded (and which had fought so valiantly) consisted mainly of convicts and deserters. They had fought well, however, and as the survivors were led away, they sang the praises of the Emperor and his knights.

The Brother Battle troops led me straight to Don Siccaro, who denounced me for not having told him about my time among the Kurgans. Gagging me after I tried to protest my innocence, he ordered my summary execution. Before he could cock his slug gun, however, the Brother Battle commander for the region, Brother Amestreus, rode up on a majestic Aragon destrier. He forbade the execution, insisting instead that Don Siccaro explain why he had sent Brother Battle troops on what would have been little more than a suicide mission were it not for my troops' heroism.

Their argument grew heated, and I could see Don Siccaro struggling to control his temper. When I finally managed to work past the gag, I shouted to Brother Amestreus to search Siccaro's tent for stolen relics. Don Siccaro turned and fired at me, though his anger disrupted his aim. I managed to twist my body so that the slug only tore into my shoulder, and Brother Amestreus struck him down with his sword. His blow must have been harder than any of us thought, for as Don Siccaro fell to the ground, his head exploded much as Purga's had a month before.

We discovered St. Belchair's scepter in Don Siccaro's tent, along with several other odd objects I turned over to Brother Amestreus. I would have liked to have turned them over to the Eye, but as the highest-ranking officer present, Brother Amestreus could do with them as he willed. In any case, I continued to serve with Duke Bellosyte's legions. He eventually granted me Don Siccaro's lands on Hira, as well as more in the lands we captured. Consequently, I must ask you to extend my leave from the Questing Knights until such a time as I can put my affairs in order. I also hope to learn why Don Siccaro risked so much for the scepter, though some writings indicate that it might allow its wielder to see beyond jumpgates. I hope that we can someday use this scepter, and that these lands may help other Questing Knights venture forth into unknown space.

Other Holdings

House Chauki had interests on many worlds, and we inherited them during the Fall. While the disruptions the Fall caused have prevented us from enforcing all of our claims, we own fiefs throughout the Known Worlds. While the lords on all these worlds do not necessarily follow all requests that come out of Aragon, they are still our brothers and sisters.

Byzantium Secundus

During my stints on Byzantium Secundus, I have heard many slurs against my house, but the same citizens who complain about our actions during the Emperor Wars are more than willing to take our firebirds. The al-Malik and we have always been the closest houses to this system, and our interest in its well being is obvious. Unfortunately, our actions have not always promoted a state of well being.

We have invaded it twice, once to drive off the barbarians who seized it during the Fall and once during the Emperor Wars. Each time we made our own claim to ownership, only to have it denied by other factions. We have also supported various local factions, especially House Lambeth. We now recognize Byzantium Secundus as the Imperial throne world, and most of us believe it serves humanity best in that role.

Still, we remain one of the largest landowners on the planet. While other nobles, especially those of Houses Shelit, Lambeth, Torenson and Xanthippe, administer much of our property, it belongs to us nonetheless. Perhaps our most obvious holdings are the Manx shipyards, which have built some excellent spaceships. While demand initially slowed after the Emperor Wars, the shipyards recently began turning out vessels for the Kurgan front. We can only hope that the same accidents that have plagued the Novgorad yard do not strike here.

While our trust in the Emperor grows with every day, you once commented to me that the main reason for Hazat influence on Byzantium Secundus is as a check against any Emperor who might want to extend his power in our direction. I believe this is true, but these holdings are not our most militaristic ones. Indeed, our fiefs on Byzantium Secundus are among our most profitable, and firebirds from their industries, farms and services help fund our war effort against the Kurgans. Duke Jose Alfonso Louis Eduardo de Aragon, who lives in some of the finest mansions on the planet, once assured me that we hope to use these holdings to promote peace on Byzantium Secundus (and, by extension, on Sutek and Aragon) while supporting hostilities against the Kurgans.

Holy Terra

During the Second Republic, and even during parts of the Diaspora, House Chauki sought to extend its influence back to our planet of origin. It bought up land in a number of different regions, but concentrated on the western hemisphere, especially its southern continent. This region had some of Holy Terra's last untouched regions, and the Chaukis insisted that these areas be left untouched.

The Church found itself in regular conflict with House Chauki, and appreciated our efforts to keep them under control. When we finally moved against our one-time benefactors, the Church aided our mission, and the fiefs on Holy Terra quickly came under our control. Of course, we then established churches and cathedrals wherever we could, and did our best to promote the Prophet's teachings throughout our lands. As a result, our people are among the most faithful on this most holy of worlds.

However, when we sought to spread our influence across the planet, the Church did move to stop us. Armed conflict never took place, but priests within our own fiefs preached a more pacifistic doctrine. In addition, before we could spread our control beyond those regions we already owned, a synod declared the planet the property of all humanity and the Pancreator, to be overseen by their servant, the Patriarch. We remain one of this planet's largest landowners as well. Our holdings even extend to Holy Terra's moon.

Pentateuch and Artemis

After being blocked on Holy Terra, my ancestors made themselves felt on these two worlds. While neither features much in the way of wealth, both have many positive attributes, as well as very capable inhabitants. We began here by buying up land, an action which lead to another synod declaring these as Church lands. We objected to this declaration at first, but when the Church demonstrated the holiness of these planets, and both House Li Halan and House Hawkwood sent in warships to support the synod, we backed off.

I visited both these planets shortly after joining the Questing Knights and had the good fortune to encounter Philosophus Antonia de Cadiz. This priest has made quite a name for himself in arcane studies, and he encouraged me to clear my parents' names. He also joined me for a tour of both worlds, introducing me to learned scholars wherever we went. Due to his efforts, and those of a number of similarly inclined Hazat, our fiefs on these worlds are both educated and faithful. These are not the warlike lands some of our detractors make them out to be. Instead, they are among our most peaceful estates, though they do have their moments. Philosophus Antonia and I became embroiled in a pitched battle against several Incarnates who sought one of his ancient manuscripts, and only the combination of my sword and his theurgy drove them off.

Obun (Velisimil)

I have always regretted the fact that so few aliens make their homes in Hazat space. I have always enjoyed the unique views and thoughts that could only come from a non-human brain, but our lands offer little chance at this kind of discourse. As I result, I have enjoyed what few trips to Obun (known as Velisimil to its natives) that I have been able to make. We obtained a fair amount of land here following the rescue of Byzantium Secundus at the end of the Second Republic, but have seen little success in expanding our holdings.

House Hawkwood has long opposed any such extension. Local nobles have charged that any lands we took would be turned against them, and that we had no appreciation for the Ur-Obun of the world. While I do not believe our strength here would ever constitute a real threat against the Hawkwood, I do have to consider the second charge very seriously.

My relatives on this world seem to have little interest in the rare treasure that is the Ur-Obun. Most treat their fiefs here as if they were on Aragon or Sutek. Still, those Hazat who have grown up among the aliens do act differently from those born elsewhere. Obun's Hazat are far more interested in diplomacy, though whether this is a result of their own tenuous position on the world or due to Ur-Obun influences, I cannot say.

Tethys

While our fiefs on Byzantium Secundus seem geared more toward income than war, those on Tethys remain in a high state of military readiness. Keeping strong military forces here provides yet another balance against someone misusing imperial power as well as a factor in pressing our claims in this system. While the solar system and much of Tethys itself are yours, some solar items remain contested. Finally, following my own experiences here preparing for my journey through Hazat space, I became convinced that a strong show of force may well be the only way to deal with many of the planet's bureaucrats.

Severus and Cadiz

While we have long owned some land on these two worlds, as we do everywhere, our estates grew during the last years of the Emperor Wars thanks to Decados gifts and trades. These deals helped confirm our alliance against you. The Decados received similar fiefs in our space, especially on and around Sutek.

I only visited these worlds once, but during that one excursion, the differences between our territory here and on other worlds particularly stood out. The serfs seem more sullen, and the nobles more wary. The estates also do not seem as productive as our other lands, though whether this is due to our management, serf incompetence or the poor quality of the land, I cannot say.

Khayyam

We have long tried to penetrate past Hira to the Kurgan lands beyond, and only recently have we succeeded. Khayyam, the system just beyond Hira, has sought to maintain its independence from the Caliphate for many years. We offer the means to keep it free from the Caliph forever, but I believe that its leaders question our motives. Still, they have given us a small embassy there — one that my house is trying to keep as secret as possible from the Caliph.